Donald MacKenzie and The Murder Room

>>> This title is part of The Murder Room, our series dedicated to making available out-of-print or hard-to-find titles by classic crime writers.

Crime fiction has always held up a mirror to society. The Victorians were fascinated by sensational murder and the emerging science of detection; now we are obsessed with the forensic detail of violent death. And no other genre has so captivated and enthralled readers.

Vast troves of classic crime writing have for a long time been unavailable to all but the most dedicated frequenters of second-hand bookshops. The advent of digital publishing means that we are now able to bring you the backlists of a huge range of titles by classic and contemporary crime writers, some of which have been out of print for decades.

From the genteel amateur private eyes of the Golden Age and the femmes fatales of pulp fiction, to the morally ambiguous hard-boiled detectives of mid twentieth-century America and their descendants who walk our twenty-first century streets, The Murder Room has it all. >>>

The Murder Room
Where Criminal Minds Meet

themurderroom.com

T0345493

Donald MacKenzie 1908–1994

Donald MacKenzie was born in Ontario, Canada, and educated in England, Canada and Switzerland. For twenty-five years MacKenzie lived by crime in many countries. 'I went to jail,' he wrote, 'if not with depressing regularity, too often for my liking.' His last sentences were five years in the United States and three years in England, running consecutively. He began writing and selling stories when in American jail. 'I try to do exactly as I like as often as possible and I don't think I'm either psychopathic, a wayward boy, a problem of our time, a charming rogue. Or ever was.'

He had a wife, Estrela, and a daughter, and they divided their time between England, Portugal, Spain and Austria.

Nobody Here by that Name

Donald MacKenzie

An Orion book

Copyright © The Estate of Donald MacKenzie 1986

The right of Donald MacKenzie to be identified as the author of this work has been asserted in accordance with the Copyright, Designs and Patents Act 1988.

This edition published by
The Orion Publishing Group Ltd
Orion House
5 Upper St Martin's Lane
London WC2H 9EA

An Hachette UK company
A CIP catalogue record for this book is available from the British Library

ISBN 978 1 4719 0547 6

www.orionbooks.co.uk

For Tony and Lucinda

I

It was half-past eleven at night and snowing when the couple left the Jamaican restaurant. Maggie Sanchez turned up the collar of her lodencloth coat and shivered theatrically. She was twenty-eight years old, six feet tall and weighed one hundred and thirty-nine pounds. She had the green eyes and smooth black hair of her Galician father and the Mayan bone structure of her maternal grandmother. She was slightly knock-kneed, a defect that was no bar to her being one of the highest paid models in England. Schools in Guatemala and Switzerland had spiced her English with an accent that was difficult to trace. Men found it seductive.

The pair had eaten wild mushroom pie and curried goat. 'Indigestion Palace,' George Drury complained, beating his chest. He handled exotic food less happily than his girlfriend. His voice was pure South London. He was ten years older than his companion and a couple of inches shorter. His hair was the colour of young carrots and styled so that it covered his ears. Crocodile shoes marred the simple elegance of his Huntsman suit. He unlocked the door of the black Lamborghini and walked around to the other side. His overcoat was lying on the rear seat.

She turned her head, looking at him through half-closed eyes. 'If you ever leave me, I'll kill you,' she said, smiling.

He switched on the ignition. 'We're long-lived, we Drurys. Fasten your seatbelt.'

The snow was falling in earnest by the time they reached Cresswell Place. It was a fairly short street with cobblestones and strips of tarmac in front of the house doors. Maggie Sanchez's home was built of red brick and tiles. The front door

1

bore a large brass lion knocker. Daffodils were growing in the terracotta jardinière. Maggie waited as Drury raised the garage door and turned on the lights inside. A smaller door led to the hall. The sitting room walls were covered with Belgian fabric. A large photograph of the model by Kirstie Raven hung above the mantelpiece. It showed Maggie Sanchez posing in front of the lion house in the Jardin des Plantes and had won the Photographers' Society award for 1984. The sitting room furniture was bleached pine; the sofa and matching chairs were French. This was a small house with the sitting room, kitchen and cloakroom below, two bedrooms and bathroom above.

Drury paused at the bottom of the stairs, puzzled by what he saw. 'Did you leave the bedroom lights on?' he called.

Maggie answered from the kitchen. 'You were last to come down.'

He ran up the stairs and stopped dead, looking into the bedroom. What he saw was a shambles. Clothes, make-up and underwear had been dumped on the floor and the cane-headed bed. He backed out to the landing.

'You'd better come up!' he yelled. 'We've had visitors!'

She flew up the stairs, covering her mouth with a hand as she viewed the havoc. 'Oh no!' she wailed, looking round the room with dismay. Her first move was to one of the wardrobes. She reached up to the shelf, retrieving a patent-leather jewellery box. Her face was tragic when she turned. 'They've taken my jewellery.'

He put an arm around her shaking shoulders. The heavy-duty nylon bags that had contained her furs were empty. He led her down to the sitting room and poured her a glass of brandy. His gaze found the empty space on the mantelpiece.

'They've nicked the clock,' he said. It was his Christmas present to her.

She drank the brandy in one swallow. 'Bastards!' she said with feeling.

He picked up the phone and called Chelsea Police Station, watching her closely. Normally she had the poise of a panther. This was a different woman, frightened and outraged. A voice

2

came on the line. 'I want to report a burglary.'

'Your name, sir?'

'The name is Sanchez. Miss Maggie Sanchez. Ten Cresswell Place, SW10. They've taken a lot of furs and jewellery.'

There was a pause then the voice was back. 'Don't touch anything, sir. CID's on its way.'

Drury wiped Maggie's eyes with his handkerchief, trying to console her. 'Don't worry, darling, at least you're insured.'

It was clearly the wrong thing to say. She brushed his hand away impatiently.

'For God's sake, George! Do you think that money's going to replace my grandmother's jewellery!'

He moved to the window, hearing a car outside. Maggie jumped as someone let the heavy door-knocker fall. Drury ushered in two men. The older made the introductions.

'Detective Inspector McGuire. This is Detective Sergeant Mullion.'

Both officers wiped their feet on the mat. The inspector was an ox-jawed man with prominent teeth and wearing a nylon raincoat and black Homburg. His partner carried a small leather case.

McGuire wiped his lips over his teeth in a smile for Maggie, his narrow eyes roving from her face to the photograph on the wall. He was clearly impressed.

'I'm sorry about this, miss. Have you made a list of the stolen property yet?'

Drury answered for her. 'Miss Sanchez hasn't had time to make lists. We only just got back from supper.'

McGuire swung round, making a full inspection of Drury. 'And your name is?' he asked pointedly.

'Mr Drury lives here,' Maggie said quickly.

The news seemed to aggravate the officer's disapproval. He took his colleague out to the hall and had a word with him. The sergeant thudded upstairs. McGuire came back to the sitting room.

'Let's start at the beginning, shall we? You say you'd been out. When exactly did you discover that you'd been robbed?'

Once again it was Drury who answered. 'About twenty minutes, half an hour ago. There was no sign of a break-in. First thing we saw was the mess in the bedroom.'

McGuire ignored him, nodding at the windows. His notebook was out. 'Are the windows fitted with locks, miss?'

Maggie was on the sofa, sitting with her knees close together, smoking nervously.

'Yes. My insurance people insisted on it when I first moved in.'

McGuire took a look at the windows. 'I notice you've got a burglar alarm. Was that switched on?'

'No, it wasn't,' said Drury. 'A dog barks half a mile away and the thing goes off. We've been getting complaints. The people who fitted it are supposed to be coming round to take a look.'

McGuire glanced up from his notepad. 'Do you mind letting the lady answer the questions?'

'Yes, I do mind,' Drury said easily. 'Miss Sanchez is in no condition to answer questions.'

'I'm all right,' Maggie insisted. 'I just want to get this thing over.'

'I can understand that,' said McGuire. 'Where were your furs and jewellery kept? Upstairs, I suppose.'

'In our bedroom,' she said. 'There's only one thing missing down here. A carriage clock.' She looked from the empty mantelpiece to Drury.

'It was a bracket clock, in fact,' he said. 'Mahogany-cased.'

'I see.' The inspector's grin was sarcastic. 'Are you an expert on clocks?'

'Just this one,' said Drury. 'I happen to have bought it.' He took a receipt from the bureau and read the particulars from it. 'Mahogany-cased, arched brass dial and subsidiary dials, false pendulum and date aperture. Made by Josiah Emery, seventeen sixty-two.'

The two men stared at one another for a few seconds. McGuire slipped his notebook in the pocket of his raincoat.

'Let's take a look upstairs.'

The sergeant was on his knees on the landing, lifting

fingerprints from the bathroom door.

'What have you found?' asked McGuire.

The sergeant lumbered to his feet. 'Not a lot. It looks like a key job. The window fastenings are intact.'

The inspector stood in the bedroom doorway, surveying the disorder. 'They've given you a right turnover, haven't they?' he said, shaking his head.

Powder clouded the patent-leather jewellery box. The sergeant had already checked it for prints. Maggie's nightdress was lying on the bed next to Drury's pyjamas. McGuire's mouth became thin and closed.

'That's where I kept my furs.' Maggie pointed at the containers in the cupboard.

'What sort of furs were they?' There was a picture of Drury on the table at Maggie's side of the bed. McGuire picked it up and looked at it.

She bent gracefully, retrieving the lingerie from the floor. 'A lynx jacket and a sable wrap. They're insured for fifteen thousand pounds.'

McGuire replaced the photograph. 'Fifteen thousand.'

Drury cocked his jaw. 'Look, can't we get this thing wrapped up? You can see that Miss Sanchez is tired.'

'We're all tired,' the detective replied. 'I could be wrong, Mr Drury, but you don't seem to have a great deal of respect for the police.'

'I've got as much respect for them as they have for me,' said Drury. 'I'll say it again. Miss Sanchez would like to go to bed.'

'Go on down to the car,' McGuire said to his partner. 'I'll take care of the rest of it.'

They heard the front door open and close. McGuire indicated the smaller bedroom.

'Who sleeps in there?'

Maggie had recovered her poise and dealt with him confidently.

'People who come to stay. Guests.'

'How about you,' McGuire said to Drury. 'Did you lose any property ... sir?' He delayed the title long enough to insult.

Drury shook his head. 'Not as far as I know. But anything that happens in this house concerns me. I live here, remember?'

'Of course,' said McGuire. 'Let's go downstairs, shall we?'

They continued the interview for the next ten minutes, Drury sitting next to Maggie on the sofa, McGuire standing. Maggie closed her eyes and yawned openly.

'I'm sorry,' she said, 'but I do have to work in the morning.'

'We'll get you to bed,' the detective promised. 'How about you, sir, do you have to work?'

Drury's face reddened. 'Yes, mate, I do. Lavender Hill Motors. You'll find the address in the phone book.'

McGuire had a habit of glancing away before returning the full force of his gaze to the subject.

'I've got a value of approximately fifty thousand pounds on the missing property. Would you say that's correct, miss?'

'I suppose so.' Her voice was tired. 'I think that's about the insurance value, anyway.'

McGuire changed course abruptly. 'Who does your cleaning here?'

'Some people called Chelsea Valeting. They come twice a week for three hours, on Thursdays and Mondays.'

'And do these people have a key to the house?'

She yawned again. 'Only if we're away. It's always returned.'

The inspector pulled a face. 'There's nothing to stop them having one cut.'

'It's a Banham lock,' put in Drury. 'They couldn't have a key cut without a letter of authority.'

McGuire nodded heavily and looked at his watch. 'Well, that about does it. We'll be in touch if anything else comes up, Miss Sanchez. You can tell your insurance company to contact me if they want to.'

Drury led the way out to the hallway. He was about to open the street door when he heard Maggie make a noise between a gasp and a cry. Drury swung round in time to see the detective stepping smartly away from Maggie. Her face flamed with fury.

'What's going on?' Drury demanded, looking from one to the other.

'We seem to have a policeman who can't keep his hands to himself,' Maggie said with distaste.

The detective was totally unconcerned. 'Just open the door. She's hallucinating.'

Drury grabbed him by the throat and pinned him against the wall. 'You can't get away with that kind of stuff, not in this house you can't,' he snarled.

Fear showed on the detective's face as he struggled to breathe, his eyes bulging. Maggie was clinging to Drury's back, beating him about the shoulders with clenched fists.

'Stop it, George, *stop* it!'

Drury let the cop go and jerked the door open. 'Out!' he ordered.

McGuire straightened his tie, his eyes malevolent. 'I could do you for this.'

'Just try it,' warned Maggie.

McGuire inched past Drury and took his place in the car beside the driver. He wound down his window.

'We'll be seeing one another again,' he called.

Drury slammed the door on him and looked at Maggie. She managed a shaky smile.

'OK, Sir Galahad, let's go to bed!'

2

It was eleven o'clock in the morning when a dark blue Saab drew up in front of Lavender Hill Motors. The man who emerged from the car was six feet four inches tall with the beanpole build of a basketball player. A beaver hat was pulled low over his ears. The hair left outside was grey streaked with blond. He was wearing a Hudson's Bay Company lumberjacket. A vicious-looking Alsatian lunged to the end of its chain as John Raven's feet crunched the cinder path between the lines of parked cars. A mobile home beyond served as an office. Raven rapped on the door and pushed in.

George Drury removed his feet from the basketweave chair. 'Hi!' he said, looking up at his visitor.

Raven lifted a hand. 'Hi!' He hung his lumberjacket on a hook and cranked himself down into the chair. The Trail Blazer had the usual show furniture with fake wood panelling and a blown-up portrait of Maggie Sanchez. Utility lines provided the trailer with power and telephone.

'Coffee?' said Drury and came to his feet, an elegant figure in a silk shirt, blue suit and black brogues. He walked through to the kitchen area. A pot of coffee was already brewing on the stove. He spoke with his back turned. 'Cream and sugar?'

'Both, said Raven. Their friendship went back eight years. The Cockney was loyal, intolerant and generous, a man whose word was bankable. His background and macho approach had made him popular among the ladies who frequented Annabel's, Stringfellows and Tramp. Meeting Maggie had removed him from circulation.

Drury returned with two mugs, gave one to Raven and sat down opposite. 'Did you ever hear of a copper called McGuire?

A detective inspector out of Chelsea nick?'

Raven searched his memory and drew blank. The coffee was too hot to drink. He put the mug on the floor by his side.

'No,' he said, 'why?'

'We had the burglars in a couple of nights ago. They cleaned Maggie out. Jewellery, furs, the lot. All she's got left is what she's wearing.'

Raven's expression showed his concern. He had investigated many burglaries during his career as a policeman, but close to home it was different. Drury shrugged.

'We were only out of the house for an hour and a half. Got back and they'd been and gone.'

Raven lit a Gitane. 'I hope you're not going to tell me you weren't insured.'

'No, Maggie's insured all right. It's just that a lot of the stuff can't be replaced, Mayan jewellery that's a hundred and fifty years old. Maggie still hasn't got over it. And guess what, on top of all that! This cop tries to feel her up.'

It was difficult for Raven to keep a straight face. Drury's expression was one of outrage.

'This Detective Inspector McGuire,' said Drury. 'Right behind my back in the hallway. Stuck his hand on her arse.'

The coffee had cooled. Raven picked up his mug. He could imagine the scene. He was under no illusion about sexual harassment. A man once arrested left his woman prey to it from friends and police alike. But Maggie was surely out of that league.

'So what happened?' asked Raven.

'I got the fucker by the throat is what happened! If Maggie hadn't dragged me off I'd have throttled him.'

He broke off as the Alsatian outside started to bark. He hurried to the window and peeped through the curtain.

'I want you to stay here,' he said. 'It's McGuire.'

The detective came in, shaking the moisture from his raincoat. His gaze found Raven and dwelt suspiciously.

'Who's this?' he demanded.

'He's the man come to give you some lessons in manners,'

Drury said happily, winking at Raven.

The detective looked round the trailer as though searching for further interlopers.

'This is a police matter. It's private.'

'Not for me it isn't,' said Drury. 'Besides, this gentleman was a policeman himself. Mr Raven, Detective Inspector McGuire.'

The two men considered one another. McGuire gave his buck teeth a wipe of the lips and shrugged.

'You want your dirty washing done in public it's your business.'

'Dirty washing?' Drury's good-looking face was puzzled. 'What are you talking about?'

The detective seemed to be enjoying himself. 'I'm talking about the burglary at Miss Sanchez's house. I've got reason to believe that you've been withholding information.'

'Withholding information?' Drury repeated. He stared hard at the cop before transferring the look to Raven. He took one of Raven's cigarettes and lit it. 'What's that supposed to mean?'

The detective lounged nearer the blown-up picture of Maggie, cocked his head and considered it.

'Those prints we took at the house, we ran them through the machine and what do you know? The Cockney playboy was convicted of theft, March the eleventh, nineteen seventy-four, Knightsbridge Crown Court.'

It was news to Raven but his face betrayed no emotion. Drury's colour heightened.

'That was twelve years ago. What's it got to do with the burglary?'

'I can tell you that,' McGuire said patronisingly. 'Fifty thousand pounds' worth of property was stolen from a house where you were staying.'

'The house where I live,' Drury corrected.

The detective grinned. 'Does Maggie know that you've got a criminal record?'

'The name is Miss Sanchez.' Drury was having difficulty in controlling his temper. 'What exactly is it that you want here, McGuire?'

McGuire bared his teeth. 'I've had a phone-call from your girlfriend's insurance brokers. Thornton and Peat. I told them that I wasn't answering their questions until I got a fuller statement from you.'

Drury made no secret of his antagonism. 'A statement about what?'

McGuire continued unperturbed. 'Well, for one thing, I'd be interested to hear why you drink in pubs with the people who clean Miss Sanchez's house.'

Drury's face was a mask of amazement. 'You've got to be kidding! You're really scraping the bottom of the barrel, aren't you! I took those guys to the pub on one occasion last summer. It was a hot day and there was no beer in the fridge.'

The detective belted his raincoat. 'You can tell me about it tomorrow afternoon. I'll expect you at two-thirty sharp, Chelsea Police Station. I'm sure you know where that is.' He grinned across at Raven. 'Nice to meet you, squire.'

The dog's barking pursued the inspector across the forecourt. Drury watched the police car drive away and kicked the door shut.

'What do you think of that?'

Raven pushed his long legs nearer the gas-heater. His tone was more curious than condemning.

'I never knew you'd been busted, George.'

The dog was still yelping. Drury bawled from the window and swung round to Raven. 'You mean I should have told you?'

Raven shook his head. 'I can't see any reason why you should.'

Drury poured himself more coffee. 'Let me tell you about it anyway. It happened when I first came here. Someone called Morry Tate came in with a Jaguar he wanted to get rid of. It was a clean motor and he was asking four and a half. That was just about the book price so I bid him four and he took it. Are you following what I'm saying, John?'

'It doesn't exactly tax my imagination,' Raven said mildly. 'You're making five hundred pounds profit.'

'Correct,' said Drury, 'that's on the book price. As it happens

I sold it two days later to this woman doctor from Clapham. She gave me four seven fifty. So round I go to Tate and give him his four grand.'

'Hold on,' said Raven. 'You mean you hadn't paid him yet?'

For some reason the question seemed to irritate Drury.

'Of course I hadn't paid him. This business, you use other people's money as long as you can. Anyway, he copped my cheque and I thought no more about it. Then guess what!'

'Tell me,' said Raven.

'The woman who bought the car is Tate's doctor. He goes round to her surgery with a bellyache and there's the Jag sitting outside her house. So he asks her how much she paid for it and she tells him. Next thing you know he's round here shouting the odds about being conned and demanding half the profit. There's no way I could agree to that and I told him so. He has me nicked, would you believe!'

'For what?'

'Stealing as bailee. A bloody liberty! What about the Stock Exchange? They're dealing all the time in stuff they haven't paid for. Anyway, I got myself a mouthpiece, a QC who tells me we can't lose. Where's the proof of intent and so forth. Anyway, I come up in Knightsbridge Crown Court in front of someone called Judge Flood. You ever heard of him?'

Raven smiled. 'Frequently. And never in complimentary terms.'

'A right bastard,' Drury said with feeling. 'Anyway, there we are with the lady doctor and Tate giving evidence. She's straight-forward but he's putting on an act. The geezer's been sucking forty cigarettes a day for thirty years and suddenly his lungs are bad. He's talking in a whisper. He trusted me, he said, gave me the keys to the car and the papers. He said I promised him that we'd split whatever profit was made. When he asked for his money I told him to fuck off!'

'And they found you guilty?'

'Damn right they found me guilty. After that judge's summing-up they'd have found Jesus Christ guilty!' Drury put on a plummy upper-class accent.

'"You are the judge of fact, ladies and gentlemen of the jury! What the prosecution says is that the defendant stole a Jaguar motor-car while acting as bailee. In simple terms he disposed of someone else's property meaning to retain the proceeds. Mr Tate tells you that he parted with the vehicle without first securing payment for it. This is something that people of common sense may think ill-advised, knowing what one does about the world of second-hand car dealers."' He tired of the accent and lapsed into Cockney. 'Six months' imprisonment suspended for two years.'

'What happened to the car?' queried Raven.

The recollection soured Drury's face. 'The car wasn't mine to sell, remember. I gave the woman her money back. She kept the car and Morry got four grand.'

Snow was sticking to the window-panes, making the interior of the trailer dark. Drury switched on the lights.

'You didn't answer McGuire,' said Raven. 'Does Maggie know that you've got a record?'

'Of course she knows! We've got no secrets from one another.'

'If McGuire does tell the insurance people you could well have problems, you realise that?'

'I know it.' Drury's mood was despondent. 'But what am I supposed to do – go round and see him tomorrow? There's no more to say, John.'

'Look, why don't we talk to Patrick O'Callaghan,' said Raven. 'He might have some legal aspect that could help. Call him!'

'I might just do that.' There was a lack of certainty in Drury's voice. The trailer was quiet except for the hiss of the gas-heater.

'I'm in bad trouble,' Drury blurted out suddenly.

'Nonsense,' said Raven. 'We'll find something.'

Drury shook his head despondently. 'It's nothing to do with Maggie or the burglary.'

'Then what?' Raven demanded.

'There's no point talking about it.'

'You already have,' Raven relented as soon as he spoke.

13

'We've been good friends for years; tell me about it.'

'I can't,' Drury said quietly.

'Then talk to Maggie.'

'Her least of all.' Drury was adamant. 'Look, forget I ever spoke. Let's drop it.'

'If that's what you want.' It was clear that his friend would say nothing more. 'Sleep on it and call me. We'll put our heads together.'

Drury opened the trailer door. 'You're good people, John. Thanks!'

The snow outside had become a brown slush that the traffic sprayed over parked cars and pedestrians alike. It took Raven three-quarters of an hour to cover the four miles home. He parked in the alleyway opposite his boat and descended the stone steps cut in the side of the embankment. The river was swollen, the buildings on the south bank dark and deserted. Lights were already burning on the motley collection of converted barges, up-river houseboats and utility craft. Not a single boat had moved from its moorings for the past twenty-five years. The *Albatross* was the last in line, built from a Victorian brewer's barge. It had once hauled barley, and hot weather still brought out the heady odour of the grain. The red cedar superstructure was forty feet long. There were two bedrooms in the bows together with a bathroom and galley. The sitting room occupied the rest of the area.

Raven unlocked the door leading to the gangplank. He knew too well that there was no way of preventing a determined assault upon his home, but barbed wire on top of the door deterred local drunks and boy-burglars. The gulls were grounded, roosting on spars and television masts, hungry and evil-eyed. He stepped into the warm sitting room, removing his shoes. Coming home never failed to give him mental and physical pleasure. The room had changed since his marriage. His wife had brought in Canadian fruitwood furniture and the chintz covers of her Ontario childhood. The fabric's bold colours, still unfaded, brightened Raven's much-mended Aubusson carpet. A sweep of glass offered on one side a view across the river, the buildings and park beyond. It was a handsome and civilised room with Raven's Klee hanging in place of honour above the stereo system.

Kirstie came from the bathroom, a tall woman with whisky-coloured hair and a band of faint freckles across the bridge of her nose. Her hair was short, of the length that Raven favoured, barely reaching to her neck. At thirty-five, she said, she was too old to push her luck. She had been on the boat all day and was still wearing the clothes she had put on that morning, an old sweater of Raven's and narrow jeans that hugged her long legs. She kissed him on the mouth and looked at him speculatively before picking up his wet shoes and dropping them in the kitchen sink.

'And what are you so hysterical about?' she asked, coming back into the sitting room. 'It's the face!' she explained.

He turned sideways. The reflection in the long gilt-framed looking-glass showed cheeks bearing the pallor of winter and shaggy grey hair. The sight depressed him. She sat down, crossed her legs and clasped a knee with both hands.

'What did George want?'

'He's got a problem,' said Raven.

She nodded. 'I gathered that much. I hope it's nothing to do with Maggie.'

'As far as George is concerned everything is to do with Maggie,' he retorted. Friends were closer than family for Kirstie, and Maggie was very close. 'Did they tell you they'd been burgled?'

'Maggie did. What about it?'

'Did she tell you what happened?'

She frowned, a network of fine lines gathering at the corners of her eyes.

'How do you mean, what happened! They stole all her jewellery and furs.'

'She didn't say anything else? Nothing about the cop who answered the call?'

She looked at him narrowly. 'I could kill you when you go into this routine. If something happened, tell me about it!'

15

He sprawled on the sofa, relishing what came next. 'There were two cops. This one was a Detective Inspector McGuire. He tried to grope Maggie on the way out. George grabbed him by the throat and had to be dragged off.'

Her mouth rounded and she laughed. 'You mean that's the problem? It's ridiculous, Maggie and a *cop*?'

The lorry-tyres that served as fenders groaned as the boat wallowed in the wake of a passing launch.

'What's so odd?' he demanded. 'You married one, didn't you?'

She touched her wedding ring instinctively. 'What I married was an *ex*-cop. You don't look like a cop, you don't act like a cop, you don't even think like one. I can't understand why Maggie didn't mention it.'

'She probably finds it embarrassing,' he replied. He fetched a can of Coke from the kitchen and pulled the tab on it.

'But that isn't what's worrying George. McGuire was over there paying a visit this morning. That's why George wanted me to be there. They found George's fingerprints all over the house.'

She reached for a cigarette and lit it. 'So what? He lives there, doesn't he?'

'But there's a complication,' he said. 'It seems that George has a police record. OK, it was a technical offence and years ago, but it's still a conviction. McGuire's threatening to put the boot in with Maggie's insurance brokers.'

Her eyebrows came together. 'I don't understand. George wasn't the burglar.'

'Don't be naïve,' he said. 'Maggie's a good-looking lady and McGuire took a fancy to her. It's pretty obvious that he doesn't approve of her relationship with a Cockney second-hand car dealer. Add that to being half-throttled and you've got your answer.'

She flicked ash with an angry gesture. 'I think that's disgraceful. The man ought to be reported!'

'For what? For putting his hand on Maggie's bottom? Of course he'll deny it. The whole point is that McGuire can make trouble if he feels like it.'

She tapped her front teeth with a fingernail. 'Did you know that George had been arrested? I wouldn't put it past you to say nothing.'

'Maggie knew, that's what's important,' he said. 'There are things that people don't want to talk about even to friends. You should know that.'

'Don't you get pompous with me,' she warned. 'I know all your hinky little secrets.'

He whistled a couple of tuneless notes. 'That's what you think! I've still got a few. It makes life interesting.' The thought reminded him that Drury was still nursing a secret of his own, one that he was unwilling to share.

It was after two when they finally sat down to eat in the kitchen, a candle on the table between them. The meal finished, Kirstie washed the plates and made coffee. He raised the glass that held what was left of his wine.

'To the woman in my life!'

She smiled, expressing her personality, warm and slightly mocking. 'You're such a deceitful rogue. I sometimes wonder how I've stayed married to you for so long.'

'No secret,' he said. 'It's because you love me.' And for once he was certain that he was right.

3

The taxi from the airport deposited Philip Loovey at the Connaught Hotel where he checked in as Dane Mitchell of Bangor, Maine. He was twenty-eight years old with the rangy build and shoulders of a tennis pro. He was wearing a Brooks Brothers suit and overcoat and a snapbrim hat over his suntan. Chote and Princeton had given him the style of a gentleman. The compassion of a shark was entirely his own. He washed his hands and face in the bathroom and unpacked his flight-bag. The room was elegantly furnished with windows that overlooked Carlos Place. He made a brief telephone-call and went downstairs again. He called his own taxi and gave the driver directions. It had been 82° when he left Palm Springs and he was cold. The driver stopped in a quiet square off Brompton Road. Iron railings and a flagged forecourt fronted a small white-painted Georgian house. Loovey opened the gate. The words WALTER ARNOLD MARINE RESEARCH (consultations by appointment only) were engraved on a brass plate on the front door.

Loovey rang the doorbell. The door was opened by a man of Loovey's own age, unobtrusively well-dressed with pale blue eyes and a smile.

'Let me take your things,' he said quickly, indicating a door on the far side of the panelled hallway. 'Mr Arnold will be down in a moment.'

Loovey surrendered his hat and overcoat and walked through the door. It was a high-ceilinged room with a view over a wintry garden where a solitary horse-chestnut tree stood on the snow-covered grass. A fire burned in a polished-steel grate. The wall-lights were on. A low table carried a profusion of current periodicals and there were some old photographs of mantas and sea-snakes. The carpet was worn, the leather sofa and armchairs deeply indented.

The door was opened by a man in his sixties with the beady-eyed aggressiveness of a robin patrolling its territory. He was bald with hair like coconut-fibre over his ears and eyes. A grey cardigan under his jacket was badly buttoned, three inches of it sagging on one side. Arnold offered his hand. The two men knew one another. Arnold opened his mouth, his tongue catching the slipping denture with the deftness of custom.

'Sit down did you have a good flight?' He ran the words together in a booming voice that was unexpected in a man of his small stature.

Loovey lowered himself into an armchair. 'I've got to admit it's getting so that I don't notice much any more. I must have flown sixty thousand miles over the last couple of months!'

'And you'd like to get down to business?' Arnold assumed the false bonhomie of a dentist.

Loovey moved his head quickly. 'If that's all right with you, sir.' They had met on half-a-dozen occasions but he never felt at ease with the older man.

Arnold lighted upon what was clearly his favourite spot on the sofa. He locked his hands behind his neck and stared at the ceiling. Whatever he saw there appeared to give him cause for concern.

'We're not too happy about this,' he observed. 'It's a highly unusual request.'

'The circumstances are unusual,' Loovey suggested. The old fogey had to crank for half-an-hour before his motor fired.

Arnold's gaze was horizontal again, his expression combative.

'There's a strong feeling here that you should take care of this matter yourselves. After all, he is one of yours.'

'The brief explains our position, sir,' Loovey said smoothly. The Brits had a hard centre that could break your teeth and your spirit. 'There's no chance of Battaglia returning to the States for obvious reasons. He's known to be using at least five different passports, one of them diplomatic. He comes and goes as he pleases. Libya, Brussels, Zürich – you name it. The one thing we are sure of is that he's going to be here in a very few days. Less than a week, in fact.'

Arnold pulled a face. 'That doesn't leave me much time. Just how good is your information?'

'The best.' Supplying the answer gave Loovey satisfaction. 'It comes from Sven Hansen.'

Arnold was clearly impressed. 'You're saying that Hansen's doing business with Battaglia?'

'Four times within the last eighteen months. Three million dollars' worth.'

Loovey suspected that Arnold already knew this. Hansen was a naturalised British subject and as a registered arms dealer certain to be the object of strict security control. 'We've managed to turn Hansen round a few degrees. There's a woman in Belgium.'

Arnold poked at the fire with an old bayonet, presenting his buttocks to his guest. The seat of his flannel trousers was well-polished.

'What about the convention, eh?' he boomed, the sound echoing in the chimney. 'No clandestine activities in one another's territory!'

Loovey swung a leg. The decision to proceed had already been taken. This meeting was simply to ensure that the old boy's shirt wasn't hanging out.

'That's why we're asking for your personal approval,' Loovey said. 'Battaglia's activities are a matter of concern to both our governments.'

'I know all that,' said Arnold, waving a hand testily. He moved to the window and watched a blackbird attempting to unearth a worm through the frozen snow. Its efforts were unsuccessful. Arnold turned. 'What about the repercussions?'

Loovey answered with confidence. 'There won't *be* any repercussions as long as you produce the right sort of individual. We'll take care of everything else. There's one thing I have to emphasise. We'll only get one crack at Battaglia. If we blow this chance, we won't get another.'

Arnold was still unconvinced. 'I'm not too happy about it.'

'I appreciate that, sir,' Loovey said gently. 'But with respect it's no longer a question of being happy or unhappy. This is a top priority project and it has already been approved. There'll be no flak, I can guarantee it. We'll have all the back-up we need. All that we want from you is the right individual.'

Arnold cracked his knuckles, firelight touching his bald pate. 'I don't see why you can't use one of your own people.'

Loovey smiled, controlling his impatience. 'That's easy. Battaglia's a guy who can hear and see round corners. He'd have been dead half-a-dozen times otherwise. And don't think he's lost his nose for danger. If there's a pro within a mile of him he'll be off and running.'

Arnold cracked his neck under his collar. 'The brief says a man with a criminal past.'

'Someone we can lean on if necessary.' This was like pulling a tooth.

'Well, we'd better start the ball rolling I suppose.' Arnold pulled an old-fashioned half-hunter from his sagging cardigan. 'Where do I get in touch with you?'

'The Connaught.'

Arnold's nose sharpened. 'Best food in London. You people certainly know how to take care of yourselves.'

Loovey shrugged. Arnold accompanied him to the street door, opened it and looked out morosely.

'I loathe this bloody weather,' he said with feeling. 'I'll be in touch within the next few hours.' He closed the door quickly.

Arnold climbed the stairs. The door to his own flat was made of steel covered with laminated soundproof material. The door had eight points of closing, two at the top and the bottom, four at the side. The mechanism was internal and there was a telescopic peephole. He was alone in the house. Young Digby was running an errand. His sitting room was sparsely furnished. A couple of tapestry-backed chairs with a table, some well-stocked bookshelves and a Chubb wall-safe. A silver-framed photograph on the table portrayed a man and a woman standing at the head of a Shetland pony. The boy on the pony was Arnold.

He lowered the slatted blinds, switched on the pedestal lamp and lifted the red telephone.

'Get me Commissioner Bannister, please.'

Arnold spoke briefly, replaced the phone and opened the safe. He carried a buff folder to the table and examined its contents for the fourth time. Folder and brief had arrived with a Home Office messenger. Each page of the brief was stamped TOP SECRET AND CONFIDENTIAL and had been initialled and annotated. Basically it was an approval of the murder of a United States citizen on English soil. Arnold's smile was wry. He knew the situation only too well. Should the exploit abort, bureaucracy would be absolved from all blame. He locked the folder back in the safe and went through to his bedroom. It had not been changed in nine years. There was a single bed with an Austrian duvet, more books and some paintings of flowers, a Jacobean chest and a small television set. It was a room in which Arnold rarely dreamed, a refuge from the pressures outside. He walked into the bathroom and anchored his denture with a squirt from a tube. His feeling of unease had nothing to do with morality. He was a bachelor two years away from retirement with a continuing sense of self-preservation and few illusions. The brief he had just read had landed on his desk as a matter of routine – it was his province as Head of Technical Services. The fact did nothing to ease his deep concern.

It was six o'clock when he heard the front door opened and closed. Digby was back. Digby had come straight into the service from university and for the moment saw his career as an exercise in derring-do. The chase was what excited him, he had told Arnold on being posted. And the chase of the human being was the noblest chase of all. It was an attitude of mind that Arnold gave a year at most.

He donned his old Raglan overcoat and Homburg hat and flagged down a cab on Brompton Road. He paid the driver off near the Embankment and crossed Battersea Bridge on foot.

The Waterman's Tavern was on the riverside, built on two levels with a terrace below where patrons sat, feeding the ducks, in summertime. The warehouses on each side of the pub had long been abandoned and awaited the assault of the property developers. Arnold descended the stairs to the snug, a bar embellished with polished teak and burnished brass. There was a distinct nautical atmosphere with pictures of sailing-boats hanging on the walls. A chow dog lay in front of smouldering logs. Mirrors reflected the firelight that flickered on the ceiling.

Bannister was sitting alone at a table overlooking the dark, swirling river. The bar was busy with the kind of people who were making the south side of the Thames fashionable. Arnold bought himself a dry sherry and carried it across. Bannister nodded greeting. His overcoat was neatly folded on the chair beside him. He was wearing a suit of nondescript cut and the sort of tie that daughters give their fathers for Christmas. A fleece of grey hair on a bony head give him the appearance of a sheep in a state of alarm. The impression was totally misleading. He had joined the Metropolitan Police Force after twenty years in the army where undercover activities had taken him from Malay to Cyprus and Northern Ireland. His promotion in the police had been rapid. At the age of fifty-four he was assistant commissioner in charge of criminal intelligence. Deeply committed, he held the view that there was no middle ground in the field of human behaviour. The rule of law was paramount. Those who transgressed it were undeserving of mercy.

Arnold twisted his lips over his sherry and put the glass down. Bannister spoke first, using the flat vowels and slightly nasal intonation of a Norfolk man.

'I've deep misgivings about this one, you know.'

'Nobody's pleased with it,' answered Arnold. 'Someone speaks to me and I speak to you. It's the way things go. We do as we're told.'

Necessity brought them together occasionally. It was too often for Arnold. He despised all forms of conventional law-enforcement and resented the need of recourse to it. He

23

was well aware that Bannister's view was equally biased. The assistant-commissioner saw the likes of Arnold as indisciplined clowns out of touch with the realities of police-work.

Bannister pursed his lips. 'Let's deal with immigration clearance first. That's Special Branch business. As I understand things, two people are coming into the country travelling on false American passports and they're supposed to be let in. Is that the way it goes?'

'Absolutely,' said Arnold. The sherry was scaling the backs of his teeth.

'Special Branch have the passport numbers. The two men will be travelling on the same plane. They're to be allowed in without fuss. Just let them through and forget about them. No interference of any kind.'

Bannister nodded glumly. 'There's a rumour that one of them has a police record. As though we don't have enough scum of our own.'

Arnold spread his hands. 'Orders is orders.'

Bannister grunted. 'I imagine that you're familiar with our structure?'

'Not entirely.' Arnold hid his total indifference.

Bannister was happy to elaborate. 'There's one man in every division of the Met who's doing two jobs. One for Queen and Country and one for me.'

'Snitching in other words,' said Arnold.

The other man was unmoved. 'I'm in the business of gathering criminal intelligence,' he said. 'I don't care where it comes from.'

Arnold finished his sherry. He was eager to be on his way.

'Let's get down to cases. Have you found someone for me or not?'

'I have.' Bannister was clearly pleased with himself.

'Then you'd better tell me about it,' said Arnold. 'This is serious business. There'll be questions to answer if the fellow's not right for the job, and I'm too old to be answering questions.'

Bannister waved a hand. 'Not to worry. This one's got your

gold star. One of my officers knows the man personally. He's an ideal subject.'

The implications disturbed Arnold. 'Just how much have you told this officer of yours?'

'How much have you told me?' countered Bannister.

'As much as you need to know.'

'That's what I've told my man,' said Bannister. 'He's come up with someone called Drury. He's got a conviction for theft and he's in trouble with the tax people.'

A look of faint distaste invaded Arnold's features. 'How would you know that?'

'I made it my business,' said Bannister. 'You'd be surprised at the scope of the new Met computers. The man hasn't paid tax in four years and he's vulnerable. I believe that was the word used, vulnerable.' He passed a piece of paper across the table. 'Everything you need is there. Telephone numbers, addresses. He's living with a woman off the Fulham Road.'

Arnold put the paper in his overcoat pocket. 'There'll be no further reference to this matter either officially or unofficially.'

'I'm glad to hear it,' said Bannister, reaching for his coat.

'I'll be able to get on with some of my own work.'

Arnold dawdled for a few minutes before walking up the stairs. There were lights in the hallway and basement when he returned to Brompton Square. He let himself in very quietly and went up to his flat. Usually he ate supper in one of the neighbouring restaurants but tonight he needed to stay close to the telephone. He called Loovey's hotel.

'Here's what you want.' He read the details from the paper. Loovey repeated them so that there could be no mistake. 'Good night,' said Arnold and put the phone down. He burned the typewritten sheet in the sink and made supper.

Drury rolled over in bed, forcing open gummed eyelids. His mouth was sour with the aftertaste of alcohol. His clothes lay on the floor as he had stepped out of them. Maggie was working in Düsseldorf and the house was no home without her. He swung himself out of bed and drew back the curtains. Snow was falling for the third day in succession. He ran a bath and soaked in it, watching the flakes on the window-panes. The thought of driving through slush to Lavender Hill depressed him. No one in his right mind would be out looking for a second-hand car on a day like this. Thought of his failing business did nothing to change his mind. Maggie had no idea of the true position. He was running on plastic, a short burst ahead of the credit-card companies and becoming skilled in the art of cross-firing cheques. Maggie was the one good thing in his life and he intended giving her the best as long as he could. Not that she cared about money, but who the hell did while you were making it! If it hadn't been for Maggie he'd have been long gone, Australia maybe, somewhere at least where the weather was good.

He shaved in the bath and towelled himself dry. He dressed in a fine woollen shirt and a pair of Italian cords. The doeskin jacket was a present from Maggie. He picked up the mail from the mat in the hall and switched on the kitchen radio. The news was depressing. Bombings in Beirut and Belfast, the promise of yet more snow. He opened his mail over tea. An invitation to the opening of a new restaurant, a reminder that the payment was overdue on the Lamborghini. He was smoking his first cigarette of the day when the telephone rang. A man spoke with an American accent.

'Is this three five one double zero double six?'

Drury hesitated. Maggie's number was ex-directory but freak calls still filtered through.

'Mr George Drury?' the voice enquired.

'I'm not buying,' Drury replied.

'Don't hang up on me!' the man said quickly. 'We need to talk. You're in a lot of trouble one way and another. I can help you out of it.'

'Who the hell *is* this?' Drury demanded.

'Never mind that for the moment. I'm sitting in a black Cadillac parked on the corner of Gilston Road and Tregunter. Be there!'

Drury stared at the phone in his hand. It took him a couple of minutes to make up his mind. He slipped into his overcoat and walked along Gilston Road to the corner. The Cadillac was parked twenty yards away. The offside door opened as Drury neared. The man at the wheel was ten years younger than Drury, well dressed and suntanned. Drury climbed in beside him and pulled the door shut. The stranger was hatless and spoke with a hard edge to his voice.

'I'm not going to pussyfoot around, George. You're in a whole lot of trouble.'

Drury fished for another cigarette, trying to control what was happening to his stomach.

'What is this, who are you?' he said.

The American touched a button. Drury's window slid down a couple of inches.

'If McGuire has his way, your girlfriend won't get a penny from the insurance company. A good lawyer could run a team through the claim.' The stranger showed good teeth in a smile.

Drury's first thought was that the man was some kind of claims adjustor.

'I'm not the one who's involved,' he said. 'It's Miss Sanchez.'

The American paid no heed. 'Then there's the matter of your income-tax. You owe the Inland Revenue a little over twenty-eight thousand pounds. Those people don't fool around. They'll bankrupt you.'

The only person in sight was a man shovelling snow from the path in front of the church. Drury turned to face the American.

'Am I supposed to take all this seriously?'

'You will if you've got any sense,' said the man. 'I'm the guy who can walk you out of the mess you are in. To be specific, I can find the money for your tax bill and I can fix things so that McGuire's report to the insurance brokers is a favourable one.'

Drury leaned his red head on the rest. In spite of the extravagance of his statement there was an air of quiet authority about the stranger.

'And there'll be a fifty thousand dollar bonus,' the man added.

Drury looked at him with fresh eyes. 'And what do you get in return for all this?'

The American's smile was guileless. 'Just a few days of your time. A trip to New York with all expenses paid. Think of it as an offer you can't refuse, George. I know all about you. You're the man we need.'

Drury flicked his cigarette through the open window, watched it fall in a spiral to the snow-covered road.

'A few days of my time doing what?'

'They'll tell you about it over there. Don't worry about a thing.'

Drury grinned in spite of himself. 'What are you, some kind of practical joker?' He fumbled behind for the door-catch.

'Don't do it,' the American warned. The humour had gone from his face, leaving flat, menacing planes. 'We're serious people. You're in possession of a valid passport. I want you to go home now and get it. Have a couple of pictures taken and take them with your passport to our embassy. Apply for a visa.'

'You're forgetting something,' said Drury. There was a perverse satisfaction in the reminder. 'How am I supposed to get a visa with a police-record?'

The skin crinkled in the stranger's suntan. 'Let me worry about that. Tell them you've got an appointment with Miss Pereira in the Visa Section. Don't forget the name, Pereira. She'll take care of you.'

Drury realised that for the first time he was taking this thing seriously. 'Suppose I tell you to go fuck yourself?' he said pleasantly.

'You won't,' the American said with assurance. 'You're too smart. Get your visa this morning. Your ticket will be delivered to the house some time this afternoon. Your flight leaves Heathrow at eleven o'clock tomorrow morning. You'll be met on the other side. From now on we'll be looking after you. You'll be back in England in twenty-four hours.'

Drury looked at him doubtfully. 'I'm not sure you're not crazy, mate. Either that or I am.'

The American's pleasantness vanished again. 'Don't be stupid, George. It's no longer a matter of choice. You're in whether you like it or not. Without us you're a total write-off, finished! And you'd better believe it. One step out of line and you can say goodbye to your girlfriend.'

Drury lowered his head, looking down at the carpet between his feet, shocked by the enormity of what he was saying.

'Am I supposed to kill somebody?'

'You ask too many questions,' the American said. 'You can call me Phil. Come on, say it – Phil!'

Drury cleared his throat. 'Phil.'

'That's better!' The American was smiling again.

'You'll find we're good people to deal with, George. Someone's going to step hard on McGuire's toes and the money for your tax bill will be in your account at the Royal Bank before you get back. As soon as you've done your job, you get your bonus, payable how and wherever you like.'

Drury found himself locking into the other man's handshake.

'Take care of yourself,' said the American. 'They'll give you a cover-story for your trip. I'll see you just as soon as you get back.'

Drury walked back to Cresswell Place. The milkman was wearing layers of scarves and mittens. The sides of his electric float were spattered with snowballs. Drury let himself into the house and stood in the hallway, heart banging in its ribcage, half expecting the sounds of footsteps to follow outside. The milkman's call came from twenty yards away. Drury went into the kitchen and made himself coffee. The events of the last half-hour had shaken him severely. He knew that such things did happen. You saw it on television, read about it in newspapers. But they happened to somebody else. He found his passport upstairs and sat on the edge of the unmade bed. The unlikely was suddenly reality and this was frightening. Being afraid was an unusual experience for Drury. He had taken to the streets at the age of fifteen with his own plan for survival. You had to be first to attack or defend, to keep your word once you'd given it and let nobody know all your business. It had worked for him but it wasn't that easy. The truth was hard to share. The thing that disturbed him most was that a total stranger could know things about his life that should have been secret. If you forgot about the cloak-and-dagger stuff he supposed it made sense. These people needed something from him and were prepared to pay for it. Looking at things realistically there was no better route to go.

He walked to South Kensington Station and had his picture taken in a booth downstairs. A taxi let him out at Grosvenor Square. The Visa Section of the embassy was thronged with people waiting to collect passports or have their applications processed. A man in his shirtsleeves and wearing rimless spectacles was talking to a security guard. Drury claimed his attention.

'I'm looking for a Miss Pereira,' he said.

The official looked at him appraisingly. 'Miss Pereira! May I ask the nature of your business with her?'

Drury produced his passport. 'I'm George Drury. I believe she's expecting me.'

The man nodded understanding. 'I see, an emergency application. Hang on for a minute.'

He used a nearby phone. Suppose it was some kind of joke, Drury thought, watching him. There was a degree of relief in the prospect. The official walked back across the lobby.

'If you'd like to come with me, Mr Drury, I'll take you upstairs.'

The two men took the lift to the third floor. Drury's guide led the way along the corridor, rapped on a door and poked his head inside.

'Your visitor, Frances!'

The room was lit by overhead strobes. A picture of the President hung on the wall. There was nothing sinister about the woman seated behind the desk. She was middle-aged with a warm smile and cap of rich brown hair. She offered an unringed hand.

'May I have your passport, Mr Drury?'

He gave her the blue-covered document and sat on the chair facing her. She donned a pair of reading-spectacles and reached into a drawer. A visa application form had already been completed with a typewriter. She passed it across the desk.

'If you'll sign your name where I've put the crosses.'

The details on the form were accurate. Place and date of birth, the full names of Drury's grandparents. The applicant was required to state if he or she had been convicted of a crime involving moral turpitude. NO had been typed in the box. He signed the form twice and returned it. For a moment he thought that she winked but it was no more than a trick of light on her spectacles. She stamped the passport and gave it to him.

'There's no charge,' she said. 'Have a good stay in the States.'

She touched a bell and a girl appeared. Miss Pereira smiled again. 'Take Mr Drury downstairs, will you, Angie?'

He waited in the steaming lobby until a taxi paid off outside. Drury sprinted for it. Once the taxi was moving, he took a close look at his passport. As far as he could ascertain the visa was the same as Maggie's and valid for multiple visits. The taxi stopped in Cresswell Place. He unlocked the door, half expecting someone to be there waiting for him. The second delivery of mail was lying on the mat in the hallway. Both letters were for Maggie. One bore the name of the insurance brokers. He placed the letters on the sitting-room bureau with the rest of her mail and reached for the phone. It was some time before there was a reply from the Irishman who had a key to the trailer.

'It's me,' said Drury. 'What's happening over there?'

The man was from Dublin and regretted ever having left.

'It's snowing,' he said.

'I know it's snowing,' Drury said patiently. 'I mean apart from that. Are there any customers?'

'There are not,' said the man. 'How about me money? Here it is Tuesday and me without the price of a pint.'

It was a subject of major concern to the Irishman.

'I gave you two weeks' wages on Friday,' said Drury. 'Borrow some. I won't be in for a few days. Switch on the Ansaphone and remember to feed the dog.' The man lived a couple of hundred yards from the yard and was supposed to keep an eye on it.

Falling snow dimmed the light in the bedroom. After a while Drury dozed. He came to his senses suddenly, hearing a whisper of tyres outside. He reached the landing in time to see something drop through the front door. The car pulled away before he negotiated the stairs. He opened the large manila envelope. Inside was a Pan-Am ticket, London-New York-London, first class. The outward flight was booked for the following morning. The accompanying letter was typed on expensive stationery.

EUROSALES INC. 551 Fifth Avenue NY NY 10014

February 20

Mr George Drury
10 Cresswell Place
London SW 10

Dear Mr Drury,

I understand that an association with our organization would be of interest to you. With this in mind we have arranged transport and look forward to seeing you here in the States.

Cordially,
David Morgenstern
Vice-President in charge of sales

Drury put the letter and flight ticket in his jacket pocket, feeling like a swimmer caught in an undertow. Either you made it to the shore or you drowned. He called Düsseldorf and found Maggie in her hotel room. He affected a jauntiness that was totally spurious.

'Hi, darling, guess what! I'm going to New York in the morning.'

'New *York*?' Her tone was incredulous. 'What on earth for?'

'To see some people on business.' He was glad that there was distance between them.

'Are you putting me on?' she demanded.

'No, I'm serious. It's someone I met, a friend of a friend. He might have something that would interest me. Look, there's no time to explain, darling. The thing is, they're paying my expenses and I'll be back on Thursday. How are things with you?'

'I'm bored,' she said feelingly. 'We shot all the interiors yesterday and we're sitting here waiting for the weather to break to go on location. Is it snowing there too?'

'It's snowing everywhere as far as I can see,' he replied. 'There's a letter for you from the insurance brokers. Look, I've got to go. Love you!'

He broke the connection, his mind bending as he stared at her photograph on the dressing table. A few hours had taken him too far to turn back.

It was one o'clock in the morning when the 747 touched down at Newmark International. Drury joined the line of clients waiting to be interrogated. He moved forward apprehensively, carrying his one piece of hand luggage. The Immigration Officer was a laser-eyed woman chewing gum. Her gaze appeared to intensify as she studied Drury's passport and visa. She fired one question after another, barely waiting to hear the answers before proceeding. How long did Drury intend to stay in the United States, where would he be living, was he in the country on business or pleasure? Drury produced the letter that had come with his ticket. The officer read it and jerked her thumb. Drury carried his bag through customs out into the concourse.

33

A man detached himself from the group of people waiting to meet disembarking passengers. He was a tall man bundled into a long winter overcoat and wearing a fur hat.

'George Drury?' he said with confidence. 'Here, let me take your bag. I've a car waiting outside.'

He led the way from the terminal building. Sodium lamps cast a ghostly light over the deserted boulevard. A lone snow-plough was working in the distance.

'My name's Kiegel,' the man said pleasantly. He unlocked a Mercedes 500 SL, tossed Drury's bag on the back seat and settled himself behind the wheel. Drury sat next to him. The Mercedes surged forward, heavy-duty tyres biting into the icy surface. The car headed north out of Newark through silent, straggling suburbs. The lights of Manhattan showed beyond the Hudson River to the east. After half-an-hour they were driving over rolling hills. Drifts of old snow glittered in the glare of the headlights. Kiegel spoke for the first time since they had left the airport. He seemed a man of few words.

'Good trip over?'

Drury nodded. The food had been excellent, the champagne free. He had sat through two movies in an attempt to take his mind off what was happening to him. The signposts flashed by monotonously.

'We're heading for Deer Lodge.' Kiegel said it casually as though the name would signify something to Drury. He volunteered no further information.

They continued their journey under a moon shining fitfully on a glacial countryside. Kiegel swung the Mercedes right off the main road, wheeling on to a secondary road that dropped between fat white hedges and through a forest of Douglas firs hung with icicles. The road ended in a clearing beside a frozen lake. A painted sign identified the rambling ranch-type building: DEER LODGE (Closed until May 1).

Kiegel braked in front of the entrance and removed his seatbelt. A desolate scene showed in the blaze from the powerful headlights. The windows in the one storey lodge were shuttered. The surrounding forest was forbidding and silent.

Wind blowing off the lake had driven the snow into piles that here and there reached halfway up to the guttering. There was no sign of life from within, not another car in sight. Kiegel climbed out, stretched his arms and stamped, his breath steaming in the sub-zero temperature. The two men walked towards the entrance, the crunch of their footsteps in the snow loud in the utter silence. Lights came on inside as Kiegel pushed the door open. He closed it behind him and drew the heavy felt curtain. It was warm in the lobby. The furniture was covered with dust-sheets.

'I'll show you your room,' said Kiegel. His shadow preceded them along a corridor decorated with pictures of cockfights. The room he displayed had two single beds covered with patchwork quilts and varnished timbered walls. A Gideon Bible and telephone stood on the table between the two beds. Enamel glimmered beyond an open door, placing the bathroom. Drury put his bag down; after a moment of uncertainty he unbuttoned his coat and threw it on one of the beds.

Kiegel spoke from the doorway. 'Let's go. There's someone who's anxious to meet you.'

Drury followed him back along the corridor through the lobby and into what was clearly the restaurant. Stuffed deer heads sprouted from the walls, a sixteen pointer holding pride of place above an empty stone fireplace. Kiegel wrapped an arm round Drury's shoulders.

'George!' he announced.

A large man in his sixties was sitting astride a leather backed chair, chin and forearms resting on the top rung. He was practically bald and wearing thick trousers and an oiled-wool sweater with a roll collar that reached to his ears, hiding his neck. Veins had broken in the folds of his nostrils.

'Hungry?' he asked, rising from his seat and pushing his hand out. 'I'm afraid the possibilities are limited but I'm sure we can rustle up something.'

'I ate on the plane,' Drury said politely.

Snow shifted on the roof and plummeted to the ground outside.

'Call me Clayton,' the old man said with a smile. 'Think of me as a friend, George.'

Drury looked from one to the other. Kiegel studied his nails ostentatiously.

'Let's get this straight,' said Drury. 'You've brought me three thousand miles to a country I'm not even supposed to be in. I've been threatened by people I never saw in my life before and now I'm supposed to think of you as a *friend*?'

Clayton nodded understandingly. 'I know exactly how you feel, George, but what you have to realise is that none of us is a free agent. Ken here's not. I'm not and you're not. There's a job to be done and we all have a part to play in doing it.'

Drury fished in his pocket, found a cigarette and lit it.

'You seem to know an awful lot about me but there are a couple of things you have missed. One of them is that I've never gone into a deal without knowing what my chances are. What exactly is this that job you're talking about?'

The two men exchanged quick glances. It was Clayton who answered. 'A man's coming to England in a few days. We want him eliminated.'

'Eliminated,' Drury repeated. So this was the bottom line. Home suddenly seemed a long way away. 'You mean murdered.'

The older man hunched, wrapping himself round the suggestion as though divesting it of menace.

'We're talking about a traitor, George. A man who has betrayed his country and colleagues. He's managed to put himself beyond the process of law but he's got to be stopped.'

Drury pitched his half-finished cigarette at the empty fireplace.

'You're talking to the wrong man. Murder's not my trade.'

Kiegel fixed him with a cold glare. 'It's anyone's trade given the right set of circumstances. What's the matter, you have moral objections?'

Drury summoned his nerve. 'I'll tell you what's the matter,' he said. 'I'm thirty-eight years old and I don't want to spend the rest of my life on the inside looking out.'

There was no doubt now about Kiegel's hostility. 'You know your problem, George, you're a failure. We're giving you a chance to shovel the shit out of your life.'

The older man broke in quickly. 'Knock it off, the pair of you. You get some sleep, George. We'll talk in the morning.'

Once in his room, Drury closed the door and locked it. He stood for a while listening. He might have been alone in the building. He tiptoed across the room and lifted a phone, getting a dialling tone. He put the instrument down with a sense of despair. He had no one to call and nothing to say. He undressed and lay in the darkness. He was in the hands of people with power. Some sort of government agency. There was no alternative.

He woke to full consciousness. Someone was banging on the door. His eyes took in the unfamiliar contours of the room. Kiegel's voice sounded from the corridor.

'Breakfast! Come and get it!'

Drury rolled from under the patchwork quilt. He had set his watch to local time on the plane. It was a quarter to eight. He padded across the room to the window and unfastened the heavy shutters. A thermometer screwed to the ledge outside gave a reading of –6°C. Deer Lodge lay desolate under a leaden winter sky. The lake was frozen solid. Black ice imprisoned a tiny island with a few pine trees. Spruce and larch crowded a ten-acre clearing. A clapboard building by the edge of the lake looked like a boathouse. Nothing moved in sight.

Drury shaved and put on his clothes. He made his way down the corridor guided by the smell of bacon cooking. Clayton and Kiegel were in the restaurant, seated at a table near a window, the remains of their breakfast in front of them. The older man lifted the lid on a chafing-dish.

'Bacon and eggs. It's still hot.'

Drury shook his head and reached for the coffee-pot. He lit his first cigarette of the day to go with the coffee. Clayton eased his silver-buckled belt.

'How'd you sleep?'

Drury moved his shoulders. 'So-so. I had things on my mind.'

Chairs were placed on the other tables. There was no sound beyond the door that led to the kitchen. Except for the three men the lodge seemed empty.

Kiegel showed his well-kept teeth in a yawn. His tanned face had been scraped clean with a razor. He looked bored. Clayton's chair creaked as he shifted his weight.

'You're scared, right?' he asked Drury. His concern seemed genuine.

Drury half-closed his eyes, releasing a stream of smoke through pursed lips.

'I'll tell you something. My father spent half his life in jail. My mother did her best to keep him there. You could say I grew up on the street. So, you do a lot of things that are wrong. But I never killed anyone. Yes, I'm scared.'

Clayton's tone was understanding. 'I'd be surprised if you weren't. You've got to get this thing in proper perspective, George. This guy is no good to anybody. He's betraying your country and mine by selling arms to people who shouldn't have them.'

Drury put his hand up. 'Don't wave flags at me! I sell second-hand cars for a living.'

Clayton's smile was benevolent. 'I've got a lot of sympathy for someone in your position. In a perfect world things would be different but there it is, you're in trouble. We're offering you a way out.'

Kiegel rose, brushing the crumbs from his soft tweed jacket. He was wearing a blue button-down shirt and no tie.

'I'll set things up,' he said shortly. He walked through the door to the lobby.

Clayton refilled his cup and Drury's and hitched his chair a little closer to the table. His voice was confidential.

'You can't afford to make the wrong decision, George. We'll nail you to the cross if you do. Make no mistake, if we have to destroy you then we'll do it. You've got a stunning-looking lady who loves you. Think about her.'

Drury pulled the ashtray near and put his thumb on the butt.

'Let's leave her out of it.'

'We can't,' Clayton said gently. 'This isn't *me* talking, George. All this comes from the turrets and domes, the people who give the orders. Try to think positively. A couple of days of your life and the slate's wiped clean. Your tax bill's paid, McGuire's off your back and you'll have fifty thousand dollars in your pocket. There *is* no alternative.'

Drury asked the question that had troubled him from the beginning. He already knew the answer but he wanted to hear it.

'Why me?'

Clayton spread his hands. 'Because you fit. It's as simple as that. It could have been anyone. You just happened to fit.'

A muffled shot sounded from somewhere outside. Clayton ignored it.

Drury shook his head. 'You're asking me to kill someone and you make it sound like you're sending me out for a bottle of beer.'

Clayton tilted forward again. 'As I said, it's all a matter of perspective. The main thing is that you understand the position, *your* position. You won't be on your own. You'll have friends you never even heard of.'

A second shot split the air in the distance. This time Clayton reacted.

'How good are you with a gun?' he asked.

Drury grinned. The question was somehow reassuring.

'I went clay-pigeon shooting last year. I fired three boxes of cartridges and all I got was a black-and-blue shoulder. That was the first and last time I laid hands on a gun of any kind.'

'A little time with Kiegel will change all that.' Clayton rose.

'Get your coat and wait for me at the end of the corridor.'

He appeared after a few minutes, wrapped in a heavy sheepskin coat and with a woollen cap pulled down over his ears. The two men stepped out into a cold that stiffened the hairs in their nostrils. Their tread cut into the crust of crisp snow. Wind knifed off the lake, rattling the boards in the building they were heading for. Clayton opened the door to the boathouse. It was almost as cold inside as out. The dirt floor was littered with the refuse of summer. Old newspapers, sandwich-wrappings and empty cans. A cabin-cruiser was suspended on block and tackle high above the slipway. Mattresses had been piled against the end wall. Propped in front of them was a plywood lifesize figure of a man. Bullet shots had holed it.

Kiegel came towards them wearing clear plastic goggles and holding a gun. He took out his ear-plugs with the other hand.

'OK,' he said to Drury. 'Let's get started.'

Clayton stationed himself on one side near the slipway. Kiegel broke the revolver he was holding, displaying the loaded chambers.

'A police special,' he said. 'It weighs just under a pound and it won't jam.' He shook the five shells from the chambers and offered the gun to Drury butt first.

Drury took it dubiously. The stock was made of walnut, the short barrel of blue steel. He was unsure what he was supposed to do next.

'Try to get the feel of the weapon,' urged Kiegel. 'See if you can reload.'

Drury's fingers moved clumsily. Kiegel took the gun again and slotted the bullets home with practised ease. He spun the cylinder and snapped on the safety-catch.

'Try again!' he said.

Both men watched closely as Drury went through the motions. After four attempts he was managing adequately. Kiegel gave him a pair of plastic goggles and ear-plugs. Drury adjusted them nervously. Kiegel had the gun again, standing with his back to the target, the revolver hanging loose in his hand.

'Start counting,' he said to Drury, 'I'll go at five.'

He spun as Drury reached the count, both arms held stiffly in front of him. With his left hand steadying his right wrist he fired five times in rapid succession. The boathouse filled with acrid smoke. When it cleared, Drury saw that each bullet had hit the target between the neck and midriff.

Kiegel winked. 'That's about twenty feet. You can go nearer.'

He moved Drury halfway to the wooden cutout. He reloaded the revolver and stood behind Drury, kicking his legs apart.

'Spread them,' he ordered. 'Balance yourself and fire, *go!*'

Drury's finger tightened on the trigger. The gun jumped in his grip. The bullet buried itself off-target somewhere in the mattresses.

Kiegel ducked dramatically. 'Jesus Christ! Look, forget what you've heard about squeezing the trigger. Take a good firm pull on it.'

Drury's second, third and fourth attempts were no better than the first. He fired the last shot. The sweat dripped ice-cold on his ribs. Kiegel reloaded the gun yet again.

'You're going to have to do better than that,' he admonished. 'This guy could be coming at you fast.'

Drury moistened dry lips. The reminder did nothing to reassure him.

'Let him take his time!' called Clayton. The cap over his ears gave him the look of an elderly delinquent.

Drury wiped his forehead with the back of his hand. 'I'd do a lot better if you got off my neck,' he complained to Kiegel.

'That's right,' called Clayton. 'Give the man breathing space!'

Drury thumbed the shells into the cylinder. This was the old routine. One guy broke your balls while the other one held your hand and asked about your poor old mother.

'Fire whatever is left in the box,' said Clayton encouragingly.

Drury obeyed. When he finished the barrel of the revolver was too hot to touch. Kiegel walked across and inspected the target. He turned to his partner.

'That makes four out of twenty-five on the mark. He'll have to stick the gun in Joe's ear.' He cleaned the revolver and packed it away in a haversack.

Drury's eyes were smarting, in spite of the goggles. He blew his nose on his handkerchief and addressed himself to the older man.

'I don't know why you have to have that clown here but I've had enough of him,' he said, nodding at Kiegel.

41

'Glad to have been of help,' Kiegel said sarcastically. He picked up the haversack and swaggered outside.

'Let's go,' Clayton said quietly. A barn-owl disturbed by the gunshots followed their exit and screeched into the trees. Kiegel was some way ahead of them, walking in the direction of a cabin beyond the lodge. The Mercedes was parked outside the cabin. Clayton and Drury made their way back to the restaurant. The older man closed the shutters, putting the room in darkness. A crack of light appeared as Clayton wheeled in a trolley from the kitchen. On it were a video machine and a twenty-four inch monitor screen. Clayton pushed a chair in Drury's direction.

'I'm going to show you some tapes of Battaglia. I want you to get this guy inside your head. Not just the way he looks but how he walks and moves. If you've got any questions to ask, shout!'

He fed a tape into the machine and switched on. A title came up on the screen: JOSEPH BATTAGLIA born ERIE PA June 9 1940 (LM/HU/CIA).

The first footage showed an airport sweltering in relentless sunshine. Heat shimmered over concrete and tarmac. Heavily armed policemen in khaki uniforms wearing the obligatory sunglasses stood by the terminal exit. Passengers were boarding an Alitalia jet. The film was in colour and shot through a telephoto lens that dragged the image close to the eye. Clayton supplied the commentary.

'Tripoli! Keep your eyes on the left of the screen, the man in the seersucker suit and panama.'

He slowed the tape, chopping the sequence into a series of poses. The man they were watching was stockily built with the combative features of a Roman senator. The eyes fascinated Drury. Black, and as piercing as an eagle's, they appeared to be staring straight at him. Clayton touched the control and the tape resumed normal speed.

'Beirut!' he announced.

The next shots were of streets lined with dusty palm trees, a corniche and the Mediterranean in the distance. Battaglia appeared on the steps of an apartment building. He looked right and left before climbing into the waiting limousine.

Clip followed clip with Clayton explaining. Amsterdam, Brussels, Algiers. Battaglia appeared on every frame. The pictures faded from the screen and Clayton switched off the set. He opened the shutters again.

'Think you'd recognise him?'

Drury answered with certainty. 'I'd know him if he wore a sack over his head.'

'Good.' Clayton wheeled the trolley against a wall. 'Is there anything you feel you need?'

'A lot of balls,' said Drury. None of this made sense and yet it was happening. The heat in the room dislodged more snow on the roof.

Clayton's smile switched on and off. 'What have you told your girlfriend?'

Drury used his handkerchief again. His nose and eyes were still stinging.

'I told her I'm here on business. I just hope she believes me.'

'She will.' Clayton put a hand on Drury's shoulder. 'She's in Germany, isn't she?'

Drury removed his hand. The weight was suddenly oppressive.

'You know she's in Germany! You know everything else, why not that?'

'Call her!' Clayton's eyes were merry. 'Tell her you're just about to clinch a deal. Women are always excited by the prospect of money.'

'Not Maggie,' said Drury. 'It's not the sort of thing she worries about.'

Clayton lifted the phone on the bar. He dialled and waited for the number to answer.

'*Breidenbacher Hof*? Hold on a minute!'

He passed the receiver to Drury. 'Miss Sanchez, please,' said Drury. 'Room eighty-six.'

'One moment, please.' It was four o'clock in the morning in Germany and the night-clerk was tired. 'She checked out last night,' he said, coming back again.

Drury cradled the phone. 'She's already left.'

Clayton's voice made light of it. 'You've got the letter we gave you. Show her that and build on it. That should do the trick.'

A car drew up in front of the lodge; Clayton went to the window. 'Get your bag,' he said. 'Kiegel's taking you to the airport.'

Drury collected his bag from the room. His return had come sooner than he had expected. Clayton was waiting in the lobby. He offered a friendly hand.

Drury took it, searching the other man's eyes. 'I want Maggie kept out of all this,' he pleaded. 'You owe me that much at least.'

'She will be.' The older man spoke with fatherly assurance. 'There's just you and there's us and that's all. You have my word on it.'

After a moment Drury nodded. 'It's important to me.'

Clayton dragged the draught curtain from in front of the door.

'Your tax bill's been paid today. And remember, help will never be far away, George. Someone will always have his eye on you. And good luck!'

The door closed behind Drury and he crossed the snow to the waiting Mercedes. He climbed in beside Kiegel.

'This is one place I'm glad to get away from,' he said, fastening his seatbelt.

The other man barely turned his head but his look was indifferent.

'Save it,' he said. 'You and I have said all there is to say. I've got other things on my mind.'

They climbed through the frozen forest towards the highway. Icicles three feet long hung from the telephone poles. Fresh snow was dotted with deer dung. They travelled the eighty-five miles to Newark in absolute silence. Kiegel stopped the car thirty yards from the terminal entrance. The place had taken on the daytime bustle of an international airport.

Drury reached for his flight-bag. The two men stared at one another for a couple of seconds then Kiegel spoke.

'Use your head and you'll be all right.'

'I'll do that,' said Drury. He walked away from the car without looking back.

The concourse was crowded with tourists on cultural jaunts, business men with despatch-cases, students carrying backpacks. The girl at the desk checked Drury's ticket and gave him a brilliant smile.

'Gate number ten, Mr Drury. Have a good flight!'

By the time the 747 started its descent to Heathrow, Drury's nerves were stretched as taut as harp strings. He had spent most of the flight in the bubble of the aircraft drinking champagne, but his mood was one of deep gloom. The Boeing touched down and taxied across to the terminal. Drury was one of the first off. He carried his bag through the green light customs area and hired one of the waiting cabs to take him into the city. They drove through flurries of snow. The streets and sky were as grey as the faces of the people. It was true, Drury thought, the English no longer have seasons, they had weather. The streetlamps were shining in Cresswell Place. Drury let himself into the house and closed the door quietly. The hallway was redolent with Maggie's scent. He tiptoed up the stairs and peeped into the bedroom. She was fast asleep, lying with an arm stretched across his side of the bed.

He undressed in the spare room and tried to sleep. After a while he dozed. Maggie woke him up with a cup of tea and the newspapers. She stood for a moment, looking down at him questioningly. The white towelling robe accentuated her dark beauty.

'Move over,' she said suddenly and crawled in beside him. He lay on his back, staring at the ceiling. She pushed her hand under his head and turned it so that they were face to face.

'What is it?' she said softly.

He moved irritably. 'I've got things on my mind,' he said. It was too late to stop lying.

'I can tell that,' she said. 'I'm not daft.'

He struggled into an upright position and picked up the cup she had brought.

'It's just that things are getting on top of me, Maggie. Know how many cars I've moved in a month? Three. And the overheads are crippling me. Rates and rent, five K a year for a poxy dump like that. Telephone, lights. A hundred a week for the Irishman. And meat and bones for the dog,' he added bitterly.

She reached across and ruffled his hair, adopting his position with her head against the headboard.

'Then sell it, for God's sake; we don't need the money.'

'And live on you?' He pulled a face.

'Have you got another lady?' she asked suddenly.

He looked her full in the eye. 'You know better than that, darling.'

'But you're so sad,' she insisted. 'I can't bear to see you like this. What is it that's troubling you?'

His story had to account for what was about to happen. Odd telephone calls, sudden absences.

'I'll tell you,' he said. 'It's this trip I've just made to the States. These people are selling cars to the American service-men in Germany. It's a licence to print money. They've got a locked-in clientèle and they get fantastic rebates. The problem is they want someone to live in Frankfurt and control the business from there.'

She shook her head. 'No way. I want you here where you belong.'

'Why do you think I turned the offer down?' he demanded. 'But there's a chance that I might be able to salvage something. They're thinking of opening up over here as well, selling to the United States Air Force bases. If that comes off they'd be interested in Lavender Hill.'

'You mean you'd run things from there?'

'I'll tell you something,' he said. 'If I manage to unload those premises I'll never look at another car again except to drive it!'

She entwined her long legs with his and scratched his instep gently with a toenail.

'I'd hate it if I thought that money could come between us. I've more than enough for both of us and you know it.'

46

He pulled her head down on his chest. 'Nothing's ever going to come between us, Maggie. Nothing in the whole wide world. These people are coming over in a couple of days. With any sort of luck that should settle matters.' He seemed to be lying as he breathed.

She wriggled out of bed and stretched her arms. 'Düsseldorf was murder. They fried me under the lights, and then had me standing in a blizzard. And all that to sell some kind of mouthwash. It's unbelievable. I'm going to have a bath.'

He reached for the phone and dialled the car-yard. The Irishman was quicker than usual.

'It's me,' said Drury. 'What's been happening?'

'The dog's got diarrhoea.'

'That all?'

'That's all,' said the Irishman.

'Get something from the vet. I'll be at home if you need me. And don't call in the middle of the night.'

Maggie was in the bath, lying on her back, her head cradled on a foam-rubber pillow. He sat on the laundry basket until she had soaped herself. She climbed out and stood meekly as he wrapped her in a bath-towel. He pulled her close and felt her heart beating. Her eyes grew even larger.

'I love you,' he said. 'Whatever else happens, I want you to remember that.'

5

Raven replaced the phone and yelled from the sitting room. Kirstie came from the kitchen, lissom in tight, faded jeans and a baggy sweatshirt with a maple leaf emblem. She touched a button, running the velvet curtains along the rails and revealing a sullen sky. It was a quarter to ten in the morning.

'That was Maggie,' he said. 'She wants us to go over there.'

His wife used a copper watering-can on the azaleas growing in the window ledge.

'Is something wrong?'

He shrugged. 'Your guess is as good as mine. She just said she wanted to see us. Both of us.'

She finished her watering and put the can down. 'Give me time to put on my face and I'll be right with you.'

He sat on a chair in the kitchen, struggling with his shoes. She came from the bedroom carrying his Hudson Bay lumberjacket and her Burberry. He got up and stamped his feet, settling into his shoes. She was at her best in time of need, although her rescue operations were mainly for the women he called her sad sorority. The Saab was parked in the cul-de-sac opposite the boat. The arts-and-crafts shop on the corner was still closed. Its owner opened when the mood took him. Raven cleaned the filth from the windscreen and they drove north to Cresswell Place. The window-boxes and roofs were plump with overnight snow.

Kirstie opened her door and shivered. 'My God, how I long for some sun. You and your promises.'

Raven followed her out of the car. Guadaloupe had been on the agenda since Christmas. He put his arm round her shoulders.

'We'll get there!' He lifted the brass knocker and let it fall. The door opened immediately.

A fine wool burnous covered Maggie's slender body. Her bare feet were stuffed into heel-less slippers. She kissed each person in turn and hurried them into the sitting room. Her eyes had the brilliance of a woman who has been crying. Her husky voice was apologetic.

'I'm sorry to do this to you but I had to talk to someone. I'm at my wits' end.'

Kirstie and Raven sat on the sofa. Maggie remained standing. There was no sound from upstairs.

'George gone to work?' Raven asked, looking around.

'No,' Maggie said steadily. 'That is, he's gone out but God alone knows where. That's what I wanted to see you about. Can I get you some coffee?'

'Coffee would be fine,' said Raven.

The kitchen door closed behind the two women. Raven could hear them talking softly. He reached for a cigarette, preparing himself for the worst. As a lady on her way out of Raven's life had once said, nothing lasts forever. It was a banality that nevertheless had impressed him. You live with a lover and wake up one morning to find a hostile stranger lying beside you. Five minutes passed before the kitchen door opened again. Kirstie detached a cap from the tray she was carrying and gave it to Raven.

'Maggie wants to talk to you,' she said.

Maggie Sanchez took the cigarette he offered her, holding her long dark hair away from the flame of his lighter.

'There's something terribly wrong with George,' she said quietly. She raised her eyes. 'Terribly wrong,' she repeated.

'You mean he's sick?' asked Raven. It was an unfamiliar role for the jovial redhead.

His wife broke in impatiently. 'Of course he's not sick! Why don't you let Maggie explain?'

Maggie's face had the brooding quality of her Mayan ancestors. 'Nobody knows better than you two how it's always been between George and me. We've just never had secrets from one another. Suddenly all that's changed. There's something going on in his life that he won't talk about. Can't talk about.'

'I'm all in favour of it,' Raven said cheerfully, avoiding his wife's glare. 'There's nothing like the odd secret to be kept. It gets the adrenalin running.'

'It's just since he came back from New York,' Maggie went on. 'He's a different person.'

'Of course he's a different person,' answered Raven. 'I talked to him yesterday. For one thing he's got a chance to unload a business he's been wanting to get rid of for years.'

She dragged on her cigarette, her long coral-tipped fingers tightening. 'He told me something last night that absolutely shattered me. Do you know that he hasn't paid any income-tax since the years before we met! He owed them nearly *twenty-eight thousand pounds*!'

Raven whistled. 'No wonder he's worried. They'll bankrupt him if he doesn't pay.'

Maggie's chin lifted. 'He *has* paid. Every penny of it. Two days ago.'

'Where did he get the money?'

Maggie's shoulders were eloquent. 'All he'll say is that it's been paid. A business arrangement, he calls it. Something to do with these people in New York. He just sits there with that silly grin pasted across his face and his mind miles away. He doesn't seem to listen to a word that I say.' She paused for a moment, giving her next question emphasis. 'Let me ask you something, John: have you ever seen George scared?'

He looked at her with astonishment. '*George*? I doubt if George has ever been scared of anything.'

'Well he is now,' said Maggie. 'And he's drinking.'

'He always drank,' Raven objected.

'But not like this. He keeps a bottle of Scotch in the car. He doesn't think that I know it. He doesn't go to work any more. He just stands at the window or sits around waiting for the phone to ring. I can't bear to see him like this.'

Raven explored his mind for likely possibilities. 'Do you think he's gambling?'

Her hair swung in denial. 'George doesn't gamble. Whatever it is that's worrying him it isn't gambling and it isn't another woman.'

He was glad that she'd got that one out of the way. A thought occurred and he voiced it.

'I wonder if the police are giving him trouble. That one who was here for instance, what was his name, McGuire?'

She sat down suddenly. 'That isn't it either. The insurance brokers called me yesterday. The claim's been paid in full.'

'Where is he now?' Raven demanded. 'I mean as of this moment. Do you know?'

She fished a piece of paper from a pocket in the burnous and gave it to him.

'I was asleep when he went out this morning. I found that on the kitchen table.'

The message was written on the back of a laundry slip. *I have to go out on business. I may be late. Don't wait up. Love George*.

He handed the paper back to Maggie. Both women looked at him expectantly. He picked a scrap of lint from his sleeve.

'I'll put my thinking-cap on,' he said. 'In the meantime don't let him know that you've talked to us.' He looked at his watch. It was ten minutes to eleven. 'Do you want me to drop you off at the studio?' he said to his wife.

She nodded and came to her feet. 'Are you sure you'll be all right?' she asked Maggie.

Maggie smiled and rose. 'I feel a whole lot better now. You're good friends, both of you.'

She looked five years younger as she closed the front door on them. Once in the car, Kirstie used the mirror on the back of the sun-visor to inspect her make-up. She flipped the visor up, satisfied.

'So what *are* you going to do?' she asked briskly. 'You didn't sound too convincing in there.'

He turned the ignition-key, bringing the motor to life. He recognised the tone of voice, the demand for some piece of instant magic that would determine and resolve the problem.

'I'll think of something,' he promised.

Her head turned very slowly. 'You think Maggie's exaggerating, don't you?' she challenged.

'I didn't say that,' he objected. 'Did I say that, Kirstie?'

'No, but I know what you're thinking. I know the way your mind works. There's something I have to take up with you.'

'There usually is,' he said, braking for the signals at Fulham Road.

'Your attitude towards women,' she said. 'If it was George worrying about Maggie your attitude would be a whole lot different. Less flip for one thing.'

'You're talking balls,' he said shortly and swung the car right.

'I've changed my mind,' she said. 'I want to go home. I have to collect some things.'

He let her out in front of the houseboat. She shut the car door with a little more fire than was necessary.

'When do I see you?' she enquired.

He moved his hand in a vague way. 'Later. I want to get hold of Jerry Soo.'

She turned swiftly and vanished down the steps that led to the gangplank. The wet snow was blowing downstream, clinging briefly to whatever it touched before dissolving. Raven waited until he saw the lights come on aboard the *Albatross* and drove to a nearby call box. It was two hours later when he parked the Saab on Eaton Terrace. The Bull Tavern was across the street. Raven had chosen it deliberately. Neither the man he was meeting nor he himself was known there. He climbed the stairs to the second-floor bar and bought a beef sandwich and a Carling Black Label. Jerry Soo appeared on time and carried his can of Coke over to Raven's table.

He dropped into a chair. 'I can't stay long,' he warned. Soo was a stockily-built Chinese with amber-coloured skin and blue-black hair. He was wearing one of the suits he had made in Hong Kong in batches of three. Each was cut in the same fashion. This one was banker's grey and was made with some unsuspected pockets. He smiled.

'How's Kirstie?'

'Kirstie's fine,' answered Raven. 'And Louise?'

Soo affected a chop-suey accent. 'She cook, she clean. So kind asking.' He lapsed into normal English. 'She's doing a concert in The Hague.' Louise Soo was a cellist with a string quartet.

Raven regarded his friend with genuine affection. The temper of the link between them had been tested over the years.

'What's it like being a detective superintendent?'

'It makes you feel vulnerable.' Soo's teeth were an example of fine dentistry and were perfect where not backed with gold. 'But I get a better chance to see what hypocrites we all are.'

Raven shook his head in despondent fashion. 'Not a vestige of morality among us.'

The Chinese rolled his eyes. 'Those names that you gave me. Is this Drury a friend of yours?'

'He is, and so's his girlfriend.'

It was lunchtime and the bar was filling up. Soo leaned forward confidentially. 'I don't have much time. I'm due at a conference. George Drury. One conviction twelve years ago. Stealing as bailee. The computer lists him as non-active. That's their stupid jargon. I doubt if he ever was an active thief.'

Raven dislodged a shred of beef from a molar, using a match. 'And McGuire?'

Soo's boot-button eyes were emotionless. 'I hope you're not involved with McGuire, John.'

Raven moved a bony shoulder. 'I'm not. Drury is. I only met McGuire once and what I saw I didn't like.'

'He's an arsehole,' said Soo. 'He's been up before two Disciplinary Boards for the same thing, sexual harassment. And he's come out each time smelling of violets. The first woman who made a complaint was the sister of someone McGuire had put inside. The other was a civilian typist at Chelsea nick. McGuire's something special, John. And to be special you've got to be doing more than you seem to be doing. Our friend's working for Criminal Intelligence.'

Raven finished his beer. 'How sure are you of that?'

'Let's put it this way,' said Soo. 'He bears all the marks. C.I. Eleven is a lot more sophisticated than it was in your time. For one thing they've got all this electronic gear. Tap alerts, bionic briefcases and so forth. And they've got a fink planted in every division. I'm pretty sure McGuire is one of them.'

Raven explained what had happened at Maggie's house.

'It's evident that McGuire hates Drury's guts. Is there any way this C.I. Eleven business could help McGuire to make trouble for George?'

Soo thought for a moment. 'You say the insurance company is paying her claim?'

'That's right.'

'Then I don't see that there's much that McGuire *can* do,' said Soo. 'They're cannibals, after their own. They're not really interested in the public. Unless there's a connection, of course. I mean bent cops like me leaking information to a renegade like you. Is there anything else, John? I have to be getting back.'

'No,' said Raven. 'And thanks for everything, Jerry. You must come over for a meal as soon as Louise gets back.'

Soo stood. 'We will, we will. Once we're sure that Kirstie's doing the cooking. I've eaten your *chilli con carne* once too often.' He walked down the stairs to the street.

Raven waited a while before following. His friend's assessment of the situation was likely to be accurate. There had to be another reason for Drury's behaviour. Raven crossed the street to his car and drove home thinking about Maggie Sanchez. His opinion of her had changed over the years they had known one another. She had turned up in London a leggy twenty year old with a letter of introduction to Kirstie. A few months had been sufficient to put the Guatemalan on the front page of *Vogue*. From then on she never looked back. Raven's first impression of her had been unfavourable. He had found her conceited and witless. It was only when she started to live with George Drury that he revised his opinion. What he had thought arrogance turned out to be a shyness on the verge of desperation. The gossip columnists had picked up on her association with Drury. Many of the references to them had been offensive. Maggie had retained her dignity throughout.

Raven turned the Saab into the cul-de-sac, backing in as usual. The shop on the corner was open, the Great Dane dozing in a window. Its owner waved as Raven hurried past. The river was swollen, the gangplank swaying. A light was on in the sitting room, a note propped against Maggie's portrait on his desk.

Maggie called. George phoned her. He'll be home about six. See you for supper. X

He spent the afternoon watching steeplechasing on television. He backed two winners in his head and switched off the set. Had he put his money where his hunches had been the animals would probably have fallen. He stretched out on the sofa and tried to reread *The Devils of Loudun.* He called Cresswell Place at a quarter past six.

Drury answered. 'Hullo mate! I understand you and Kirstie were here?'

'That's right,' said Raven. So much for Maggie's discretion.

Drury seemed to read his thoughts. 'It wasn't Maggie. You left your Gitanes behind.'

Raven's grope in his pocket was automatic. 'She's worried about you,' he said. There was no sense in pussyfooting.

'She told you about the tax?'

'She told us,' said Raven.

Drury's tone became salty. 'Look, mate, I don't want to sound ungrateful but I'd rather you people stayed out of all this. Maggie's going through some sort of phase. She'll get over it. OK?'

The door banged at the end of the gangplank. Kirstie was home.

'I've got a feeling that I've just been put in my place,' said Raven.

'Bullshit,' said Drury crisply. 'You'll be the first one to know when I do need help. I'll talk to you later.'

Kirstie came in carrying a shopping bag. She took a quick

look at *The Sporting Life* on the floor and blew him a kiss.

'Did you back any winners?'

He swung his legs from the sofa. 'I didn't back any losers. I just spoke to George.'

She pulled the scarf from her head and shook her hair free.

'And how did that go?'

He picked up the newspaper from the floor. 'It wasn't what I'd exactly call a rewarding conversation. He'd rather be left alone.'

6

Drury put the telephone down with the delicacy of a bomb-disposal expert. It was twenty past seven in the morning and still dark outside. The looking-glass showed no change in his appearance. He climbed the stairs like a cat but Maggie was awake and waiting for him. Sleep had reddened one side of her face.

'Who was that on the phone?' she asked, shading her eyes from the light.

'One of the guys from New York,' he replied. 'He's at Heathrow and wants me to meet him.'

'At this hour!' Her fingers fastened on his pyjama jacket. 'What's going on, darling? *Please* tell me!'

'I've just told you,' he said, disengaging himself from her grip. 'I'm sorry, darling, I've got to get dressed.'

She relinquished her grasp reluctantly. 'You're not telling me the truth,' she accused.

'That's great,' he blustered. 'What the hell is happening to you, Maggie?'

Her eyes were sad. 'If you don't know the answer to that then you're a fool.'

He bent and kissed her mouth as if for the last time. 'I'm sorry you don't believe me.'

'So am I,' she said.

She watched as he pulled on charcoal-grey slacks and a polo-necked sweater. He took his leather bomber jacket from the cupboard and sat on the edge of the bed, tying his shoelaces.

'You're wearing odd socks,' she said suddenly, pointing.

He glanced down. One sock was black, the other was blue.

'It's supposed to be lucky,' he said. 'Why don't you go back to sleep. You're not working.'

She stretched her long legs under the duvet. 'Just come home in one piece. Do that and all will be forgiven.'

He came to his feet. 'You're acting in a very strange way, Maggie,' he said uncertainly. 'I'm seeing a man on some business. I've got a chance to do myself some good and you're acting like a bloody prima donna. I'll call you as soon as I know what I'm doing, all right?'

The bedside lamp was extinguished and she pulled the covers over her head without answering. He let himself out of the house on to a quiet street under a hostile sky. The snow had stopped falling. The black Cadillac was parked in its usual place, facing west on the corner of Tregunter Road. Loovey opened the door for him. The American was dapper in a blue flannel suit and pale grey shirt. He started the motor.

'How are you feeling today?'

Drury adjusted the seatbelt. 'I've felt better in my time.'

Loovey reached across and patted Drury's knee in a friendly fashion. They drove west along the Fulham Road and swung left at Parsons Green towards Hurlingham. Loovey pulled the Cadillac on to a short driveway with trees. The redbrick house backed on to the river. It had been bought two years previously by a fifty year old female landscape painter with impeccable references. Loovey opened the front door, ushering Drury into the warm hallway and sitting room. French windows over-looked a snow-covered garden. Tall walls gave it privacy. A gate at the end opened on to the towpath. There was a view of the gasworks on the south bank of the river.

Loovey nodded pleasantly. 'Empty your pockets. Put every-thing on the table.'

For a moment Drury thought that he had misheard. 'What did you say?'

'The pockets,' said Loovey. 'Empty them out on the table.'

Drury obeyed, fumbling for his keys and money. 'That's the lot,' he said.

'Put your hands against the wall and spread your legs.'

Loovey grinned. 'You know the way it goes.'

'I don't believe this,' said Drury. He held quite still as the American searched him expertly.

'Don't worry about it!' Loovey's smile drew Drury into complicity. 'OK. We've got that crap out of the way. Let's have some coffee.'

The kitchen faced south, getting the best of what light there was. A three-day-old copy of *The New York Times* lay on the table. A half-smoked joint was stuck to the ashtray. Loovey scraped it into the garbage pail without comment. He shook ground coffee into the percolator and switched on the power.

'I'm sorry I couldn't give you any warning,' he said, looking across at Drury. 'I didn't know myself until a couple of hours ago. Battaglia gets in this evening.'

Drury tried to moisten his lips but found no saliva. He felt for his cigarettes. At the back of his mind had been the hope that something would happen at the last minute to bail him out. The hope had just sunk. The percolator started to bubble. Loovey took cream from the refrigerator, sugar from the dresser. He found two large mugs and set them on the table. Each move he made was with sureness and ease. He was smiling.

'It's time to deliver, George, but don't worry about it. Just follow instructions and you're a shoo-in.'

Drury looked at him glumly. What he had in mind was rapping Loovey between the eyes and taking off. But there was a problem there. Where would he run to?

Loovey poured the coffee and sat down across the table from Drury. 'If you've something that's bothering you, tell me,' he said.

'You just lit a stick of dynamite under my backside. That's what's bothering me.' Drury spooned sugar into his mug.

A couple of frown marks creased the American's suntanned face.

'Come on now, we've got to be realistic here! We've kept our part of the bargain. Your tax bill's settled, the cop's muzzled and your bonus is waiting. The time has come for you to deliver.'

59

A film of sweat seemed to cover Drury's body. He took off his leather jacket.

'Don't worry about me.' He did his best to make his expression match the words.

Loovey lowered his mug. 'Believe me, there's nothing to it. After the first one you don't even think about it.'

Drury almost choked on the thought. 'The *first*! There aren't going to be any others!'

'In a manner of speaking,' Loovey said smoothly. His smile was ingenuous. 'This time next week you'll be lying on a beach somewhere in the South Pacific with your girlfriend. Can you drive a Honda?'

'I can drive anything with wheels,' Drury answered. That much at least was true.

'Good,' said the other man. 'We're going to the country, thirty miles out of London. The house is near a village outside Horsham. The nearest neighbours live half-a-mile away. There's nothing but woods between them and the house we're interested in. There are two servants, a man and a woman. Don't worry about them. They've been given the night off. You'll see them leave in a white Renault. That's when you go in.'

Drury cleared his throat. 'I go in *how*?'

'Through the front door,' Loovey passed an Ingersoll key across the table. 'You'll be completely alone in the house. There isn't a dog, even. Battaglia's taking the seven-twenty from Victoria. It gets into Horsham at eight-ten. A car will meet him and bring him to the house. That's roughly a half-hour drive. Battaglia's expecting to stay the night where you're going. He'll get out of the car and ring the doorbell. *Don't open that door until you're sure that the car has gone.* Once you're certain that it has gone let him in and make sure that he doesn't leave. Is that clear?'

Drury wet his dry mouth with coffee, looking at the key he was holding.

'He's expecting someone to be in the house?'

'You're not listening,' Loovey reproved. 'Joe's expecting

servants to be there and he's expecting his host to be there. He's supposed to be here on business. *Big* business. But it's a set-up, George. The man he's coming to see is still in Belgium. Joe's been had. All you do is open the door and pull the trigger. It's not that difficult.'

Drury slipped the key into his trouser-pocket. 'How about the body?' He was surprised he could say the word without stumbling over it.

'That's not your concern,' said Loovey. 'As soon as you've done your job you get the hell out of there. You bury that key and the gun somewhere safe and drive seven miles to a filling-station. I'll show it to you on the way down. They close for business at six o'clock in the evening but there's a phone box on the forecourt. What you do is drive in, cut your lights and stay out of sight. At nine o'clock precisely, I'll call you there and tell you what comes next. OK?'

'OK,' Drury said without enthusiasm. Loovey had made it all too clear.

'Let's move,' said Loovey. He picked up a shopping bag in the hall and opened the front door.

Loovey drove the Cadillac east with confidence, displaying a surprising knowledge of short cuts and back doubles. His goal was an eight storey car park behind Sloane Square. He leaned through his window and took a ticket from the dispensing machine. The Cadillac glided up the ramp to the top floor. It was only partially walled and open to the weather. The only vehicle there was a dark blue Honda. The lift stopped at the floor below. Loovey walked across to the Honda and placed the shopping bag on the roof. He unlocked the boot and the car and showed Drury what was in the bag. There was a pair of thin leather gloves, an entrenching tool and snubnosed revolver. It was the same model as the gun Drury had used at Deer Lodge.

'The tool's for digging the hole,' said Loovey. He put the shopping bag in the boot, locked it and gave the keys to Drury. 'You drive.'

Drury got behind the wheel and adjusted the seat. 'What happens to the Caddy?' he said, looking at its gleaming shape.

'You worry too much,' said Loovey. 'Do you know your way out of town on the A23?'

'I know all the ways out of town,' said Drury. The motor started easily. A man in a booth at the foot of the ramp took the parking ticket and money from Loovey. An hour later they were eating steak-and-kidney pie in a pub near Redhill. Loovey seemed determined to confine their conversation to generalities. By four o'clock they were driving through the outskirts of Dorking. Drury's brain was jinking like a hunted hare. Every mile carried him closer to the ultimate showdown and he saw no hope of salvation.

Loovey touched his arm. 'Coming up on your right. That's the filling-station.'

Drury's foot touched the brake pedal. The two-pump petrol-station perched on a rise twenty yards from the main road. An office behind the pumps dispensed the usual soft drinks, confectionery and car accessories. There was a work-bay with a car up on the hoist, a pair of legs under it. The telephone-box was at the side of the office.

'Don't forget, they close at six,' Loovey said, glancing back at the receding petrol-station. 'I'll call you at nine on the dot.'

They continued through fading daylight. 'Take a left here,' Loovey said suddenly. A signpost read WARNHAM 3 miles. The lane descended gently past a row of brick cottages and into a wood with tangled undergrowth. After a while the lane rose again, finally emerging from the tunnel of trees. A stone wall extended on the right. Two hundred yards along was a white-painted gate and a drive through still more trees. Opposite the gate was a water-tower covered with ivy. A rutted track past the water-tower gave access to the fields beyond. Loovey instructed Drury to take it. The Honda bumped over the frozen track and stopped in front of the gate. A pony, shaggy in its winter coat, raised its head from some hay on the ground to look at them. Loovey reached over and switched off the ignition. The motor died and the silence was complete. The water-tower hid them from the road.

Loovey leaned back against the door behind him. 'You drop

me off at the station and come back here. The moment you see the Renault leave you drive in through the gates. Leave the car somewhere out of sight in the garage.' He turned his wrist, checking his watch. 'Let's go!'

The station was on the main line to London, a halt for the commuters who flocked into the city each morning. During the day it was deserted. At the moment, lights shone on an empty platform. A line of parked cars in front of the station was powdered with snow.

'Let me off here!' ordered Loovey. He opened the door and leaned back in before closing it. Drury heard the sound of a train in the distance. 'Remember he'll come at you fast,' warned Loovey. He lifted a hand, turned and walked away towards the lights.

Drury turned the Honda and drove back to the water-tower. He cut the lights and the motor and sat with the windows down in the darkness. A fox barked in the woods. Minutes passed, then came the sound of a car on the drive. Drury slipped out of his seat and inched along the brickwork of the water-tower. He could see the white gate from where he stood. Head-lamps illuminated the lane and a white car appeared. The driver emerged, opened the gates and drove out leaving the gate open. Drury watched the tail-lights dwindle. Then he unlocked the boot of the Honda, donned the thin gloves and stuck the revolver in his pocket. He drove across the lane on to the drive and down through Scots pines and beeches to a gravelled turning-circle in front of a Queen Anne manorhouse. Chinks of light showed through some downstairs curtains. The upper part of the house was in darkness. He drove the Honda under an arch into a cobbled yard. The coach-house had been converted into a four-car garage. Drury lifted the cantilever door on the elegant lines of a silver Corniche. He backed the Honda in beside it and lowered the door again. The dull thudding he felt in his chest was his heartbeat. He crossed the yard to the back of the house. Everything was very still. There was no light in the kitchen but the curtains were open. A glimmer of enamelled surfaces showed in the darkness. The back door was locked and bolted. He put his ear against it. Nothing. He walked round the house in the opposite direction. There was enough light to make out the redbrick walls and white window-frames. Snow covered the flowerbeds. He was walking on gravel again. Reeds fringed an expanse of black water on the far side of the turning-circle. Beyond that rhododendrons and azaleas merged into the trees. Drury's thin-soled loafers made little noise as he walked towards the front door. He inserted the key in the lock and the heavy door yielded. He stepped into the warm-lighted hall. Gilded figures of monks held electric candles. Seascapes on the walls climbed with the wide, shallow stairs. The parquet flooring was covered with Persian rugs. A grandfather clock at the foot of the staircase ticked away time in stately fashion. Battaglia's train was due in a few minutes. Ten more would bring him to the house. Drury saw himself with startling suddenness in the gilt-framed looking-glass – a stranger holding a gun in gloved hand. A worm of fear crawled in his stomach. Violence had been part of his life from an early age. It had ruled the streets where he had grown up. But this was going to be different. The man who would come through that door had been trained to kill, a man who lived on a knife-edge. There would be no margin for error.

Drury turned away from his reflection and opened a white-painted door. The flickering lights he had seen came from the fireplace. Coal gleamed in a brass scuttle. The table was set for two people. The cloth was damask, the cutlery silver. Drury tiptoed across the room to a table under the window. An expensively printed booklet had the name Hansen p.l.c. on the cover. He carried it nearer the fire and opened it. An entry on the first page had been marked with a felt pen. 'Two hundred reconditioned 0.55 Brownings. Stellite barrels, tripods and cleaning-kit included. Five hundred dollars (US $500) per unit. Department of Trade and Export Licenses available.'

The same felt pen had scrawled the name 'Colonel Ube Bayas' and the amount '$25,000' in the margin. Each page in the catalogue carried an offer of arms for sale.

A noise came from the direction of the baize door in the hall. He put the catalogue back on the table and hurried towards it. The green baize door opened on to a short passageway. The noise came again from the kitchen. It was the whirr of a refrigerator motor. He looked at his watch, ran back into the hallway and turned off the lights. A single lamp still burned in the dining room. He stood with his ear pressed against the front door. He heard the car coming long before it turned on to the driveway. Tyres crunched the gravel seconds later. A door opened and slammed. A man with an American accent spoke and the wheels of the taxi turned. Footsteps crossed the gravel; a bell rang at the back of the house. Drury ignored it, listening to the taxi in the lane. The bell rang again, twice in rapid succession. Drury braced himself and jerked the door open.

Battaglia was standing a couple of feet away, wearing a light cashmere overcoat. Dark glittering eyes in a deeply tanned face stared at Drury. Battaglia's smile faded as he saw the gun in Drury's hand. He lunged forward suddenly like a burly guard-dog. Drury stepped back smartly. He fired with a ferocity born of fear. Battaglia staggered, clasping his hands over his stomach. He looked down at the blood oozing through his fingers with an expression of incredulity. The second shot hit him in the sternum and he pitched forward across the threshold of the open door. The fumes from the explosion filled the hall. The echoes chased one another through the trees. Drury dragged the body inside and stepped outside, pulling the front door shut behind him.

The trees stood like sentinels. A sound came from somewhere within the house. His brain identified it as the noise of a dying man trying to pull himself upright. He ran in the direction of the garage, refusing to accept the message in his head. The gun was still in his hand. He jammed it into the pocket of his bomber jacket. He raised the cantilever door, dry-mouthed and sticky with sweat, and drove the Honda out. The house looked peaceful, firelight flickering on the ceiling beyond the curtains. He drove on, fighting his cowardice, refusing to look back as he sped up the drive. He stopped the Honda behind the water-tower, cut the lights and took the entrenching tool. He climbed the gate and ran across the field into the skeletal shapes of the trees. Brambles tore at his clothing. He stopped after a while and raked away the crust of dead leaves with a foot. The earth beneath was unfrozen. The tool in his hands cut through easily. He dug a hole large enough to take the gun, key and entrenching tool, added the doeskin gloves and scraped the loose dirt back. He scattered some leaves, and there was no sign left of his visit.

It was twenty minutes to nine by the time he reached the petrol-station. A CLOSED sign blocked the entrance to the forecourt. A light burned in the empty office. He drove the Honda round behind the work-bay and close to the phone-box. He turned off the headlamps. The memory of the noise he had heard as he left the house still disturbed him. A picture formed in his mind of Battaglia clawing his way to the phone, knocking over chairs as he went. The need to know the truth over-rode everything else. He left the car and fed coins into the slot in the telephone-box. Raven's voice answered.

'It's me, John,' said Drury. 'I want you to do something for me. Don't ask questions, just *do* it! There's a house called Capel Manor in Warnham. That's near Horsham. I want you to phone them and see if you get an answer. I'm in a phone-box.' He read the digits from the dial in front of him.

'Check,' said Raven. 'What's the number of the house?'

'I don't have it,' said Drury. 'You've got the address and you know how to get the number. And hurry!'

The phone rang in six minutes' time. 'That number doesn't answer,' said Raven. 'It's ex-directory. The subscriber's some-one called Sven Hansen. What's going on, George?'

'I'll talk to you later,' said Drury and put the phone down. He walked back to the car and sat waiting for Loovey's call. Traffic flicked by on the main road. Grit had been spread on the surface. He did his best to put the events of the last week out of his mind. It was no time for wound-licking. His confidence grew as the minutes passed. A little more time and it would all be over. He would leave the car wherever they said and that would be the end of it. He had a stake now. Fifty thousand dollars and whatever he could get for the car-yard. Everyone found himself sooner or later. All he wanted from life was to hold Maggie close and share happiness with her.

The minute hand of the dashboard clock jerked its way towards nine o'clock. He knew nothing of what came next. A kilo of plastic explosive attached to the drive-shaft burst through the floorboards, removing Drury's legs from his torso. Bloodstained splinters of bone spattered the fuel-pumps. The debris was blown thirty yards away through the smoke. The pumps exploded seconds later. The phone started to ring in the wrecked phone box.

7

The limousine swung off the lane on to the drive, headlamps searching the snow-fat trees. Ben Stepka sat on the back seat, a stockily built man in his late forties wearing a bankers' blue suit and dark overcoat with a black velvet collar. The negro driving wore a grey chauffeur's uniform and matching cap. Shaky Jake was ten years younger than his passenger. Both men were wearing surgical rubber gloves. The limousine glided on to the turning-circle at the end of the drive. Mist from the lake wreathed in the trees and clung to the soft red brickwork of the house. Lights showed through the curtains on the left of the front door. The chauffeur stopped the engine and swung round, rolling his eyes.

'Welcome to Frankenstein Hall,' he said in a sepulchral voice.

Stepka just looked at him. He was in no mood for this kind of humour.

'You smoke too much dope,' said Stepka. 'The man catches you, it's your ass. Let's get to work.'

They walked across the gravel to the front door. Stepka used a key to unlock it. The two men stepped inside quickly and closed the door behind them. The smell of burned gunpowder hung in the dark hall. A clock nearby ticked with smooth regularity. Stepka found the light-switch. The body was lying face-down, arms extended as though reaching for something. The hands were clenched into fists. Blood soaked the rug on each side of the body. Stepka rolled Battaglia over. The dead man's eyes were open, his mouth agape in a snarl. Two blackened bullet holes in the light cashmere overcoat were the sources of the blood.

Shaky Jake Mills whistled softly. 'There's one turkey ain't going to take no prizes for looks.'

Stepka ignored him. This was the first time he had worked with Mills. Loovey had vouched for him and Stepka was disposed to believe most of what Loovey said. Shaky Jake was a stand-up guy and a magician with a couple of batteries and some explosive. The reputation made Stepka nervous. He searched the dead man's pockets, taking care not to soil his clothing with blood. The haul comprised the return half of a Zürich-London-Zürich air ticket, a wallet and a Canadian passport. The passport had been issued in the name of Pierre Burenne, born in Montreal January 23, 1942. Occupation numismatist.

Shaky Jake spoke from behind Stepka's shoulder. 'What the fuck's a numismatist?'

'A five card artist,' said Stepka. 'Don't ask dumb questions.'

The wallet contained twelve hundred American dollars, eighty-five British pounds and two thousand Swiss francs. Shaky Jake extended his hand, pink palm uppermost.

'No chance,' Stepka said righteously.

Mills seemed not to have heard. He was staring down at Battaglia's body. Fresh blood welled from the dead man's mouth, dislodged by the change in position.

'This guy's still alive, man!' Shaky Jake's eyes narrowed.

'He's dead,' Stepka said shortly. 'You got problems, a good confession solves everything.'

'There's a little misunderstanding here,' Shaky Jake said. 'I'm a Muslim.'

'Whatever,' said Stepka. 'Give me a hand to wrap him up.'

They rolled the body in the rug. Stepka opened the front door. Shaky Jake lifted the legs. Stepka took the shoulders. They carried the body across the gravel and placed it in the boot of the Daimler. Stepka turned the key on it. A joint glowed in Shaky Jake's mouth.

'For crissakes,' Stepka objected. 'You're driving.'

'That's why I'm smoking,' the negro answered. 'I'm driving a stiff. Get in the back.'

Stepka climbed in. The stink of hash filled the interior of the car.

'Great stuff,' he said bitterly. 'We get stopped you've got eyes like chestnuts.'

Shaky Jake grinned into the driving mirror. 'You're a good man, uncle, but I get the urge to go up alongside your head at times.'

Lowering snow-clouds made the night even darker. Once out on the main road Shaky Jake kept the car moving at a steady pace, holding his position in the inside lane. The route they had been given took them through Reigate and Crawley on to the North Circular Road at Chiswick. Most of the traffic was coming from the opposite direction into the city. The radio was on and Shaky Jake was listening to it. Stepka was glad. Negroes always made him nervous. His time in the Federal penitentiary had done nothing to diminish his edginess. Shaky Jake was everything Loovey had promised, cool under pressure, a demolitions expert who fought through two years in Nam. What unmanned Stepka were the sudden fits of laughter in the middle of Shaky Jake's long silences.

It was eleven o'clock when they reached Newmarket. The streets were still busy, the cinemas and pubs emptying. A few minutes took them in and out of the small town. Stepka called a halt and lit a small reading lamp at his shoulder. The ordnance survey map showed the perimeter of the airfield. The entrance they had been instructed to use was at the rear of the field, four miles from the main stockade. Stepka folded the map and extinguished the light.

'Take a left when you get to the crossroads.' He looked up sharply. 'Something amuse you?'

'You're whistling again,' Shaky Jake said into the mirror. 'Every time you've got problems we get the birdsong.'

It was a habit that Stepka had had all his life but he was in no mood to be reminded of it. They skirted a barbed wire fence twelve feet high and lit by high-power strobes. An encampment of CND protesters was silent under the light snow that had started to fall. Primitive shelters had been fashioned out of branches, plastic sheets and cardboard cartons. There were a few pegged tents and people in sleeping-bags. A small guardhouse controlled a steel-and-mesh gate in the fence. A sign warned of the presence of guard-dogs.

'Pull your window down,' warned Stepka as they approached.

'Get rid of the stink!'

Shaky Jake touched the horn. A uniformed sergeant stepped from the guardhouse carrying a sub-machine gun. He loped across after his shadow and inspected the car through the mesh.

'How many you got in there?' he called.

'Just the two of us,' Shaky Jake answered. 'Me and the passenger.'

'Drive in and stop at the guardhouse,' ordered the airman. He yanked a lever freeing the locking mechanism. The gate swung open. The limousine rolled forward. Loovey emerged from the guardhouse. The sergeant flapped his free hand in salute. Loovey climbed in beside Stepka.

'Left,' he said. The concrete-topped road ran parallel with the fence. Across the waste of tarmac were the main buildings and crew-quarters. Half-a-dozen fighter planes were lined up in front. The road veered towards some hangars. The door of the nearest was open.

'In there,' pointed Loovey.

Shaky Jake obeyed. The hangar door rolled shut behind the car. A Convair C131 waited under the lights. The words Military Air Transport Service were painted on the fuselage. The three men climbed out. There was nobody else in the vast hangar.

'OK,' said Loovey, nodding at the boot of the Daimler, 'get him out.'

Shaky Jake and Stepka lifted the corpse from the boot. Battaglia's arms were still imprisoned in the rug. Loovey bent over, inspecting the death-mask closely. His expression showed nothing at all.

'Pick him up,' he said.

They carried the corpse to the Convair. A baggage hatch was open on the far side. A coffin stood on the oil-stained concrete below. The top was propped against a wheel.

'Get him in there,' said Loovey. 'The rug goes too.'

It was a tight fit, requiring the use of some force. Stepka wiped the sweat from his grizzled crewcut.

'You want the top on?'

Loovey grinned. 'What do you think? The guy's got a long ride.'

It was a well-made oak coffin with a purple lining and brass handles. Shaky Jake busied himself with the screwdriver and patted the top of the closed box.

'So long, old buddy,' he said softly.

Loovey's voice was tolerant. 'You been smoking more of that ganja?'

The negro did a little Uncle Tom shuffle. 'Just the one toke, massa!'

Loovey glanced sideways at Stepka. 'Just the one,' said Stepka. He had to live with the man and worried about his back.

'You guys get yourselves back to London,' said Loovey. 'The sergeant will let you through the gate. You know what to do with the car.'

'Leave it in the square,' said Stepka. 'Keys in the exhaust.'

Loovey walked to the hangar door and banged on it with the flat of his hand. Someone outside rolled it back. The other two men took their places in the car. The sergeant opened the gate as they neared. They were passing the CND encampment when Shaky Jake spoke.

'You're a honky mother but you all right, man.'

'Thanks,' Stepka said drily. 'I've got an idea you just fell off the perch.'

The driver adjusted his chauffeur's cap, setting it at a jaunty angle. 'You think so, uncle?'

'I think so,' said Stepka. 'The man's got your number.'

8

It was eight o'clock in the morning and Raven was still in bed. Kirstie had already left for the airport. She had an all-day session in Paris and would sleep in their *Quai d'Anjou* apartment. The phone rang on the bedside table. Raven stretched out. The voice was that of a stranger.

'This is Doctor Munro. May I speak to Kirstie Raven, please?'

'She's in Paris,' said Raven. 'She won't be back until tomorrow. I'm her husband. Is there anything I can do?'

'I'm at Maggie Sanchez's house,' said the doctor. 'Does the name George Drury mean anything to you?'

'Of course,' Raven said quickly. 'He's a friend. Both of them are.'

'He's dead,' said the doctor. 'That's why I'm here. The police have only just left the house. Maggie's in a state of shock and she's been asking for your wife.'

'Oh my God!' exclaimed Raven. It was hard to believe what the doctor was saying. 'I was talking to him only last night. What happened?'

'The officer who was here didn't seem to know much. The Surrey police had rung through and asked Chelsea to notify Maggie. Apparently it was an accident in a petrol-station outside Dorking. They say one of the pumps had been leaking and there were fumes. George must have struck a light.'

Raven stared through the window. A tug was towing a line of barges upstream. Gulls rose shrieking protest as the flotilla of boats wallowed in the wake of the convoy. He dragged himself back with an effort.

'How do they know it's George?'

'Something they found on what was left of the body. That's what they say at any rate. Maggie had been up all night waiting for George to come home.'

'Look, I'm still trying to take this in,' said Raven. 'I'll be round just as soon as I've got some clothes on. Can you give me half-an-hour?'

The doctor's voice was dubious. 'The thing is I've got a surgery at nine.'

'Twenty minutes,' promised Raven. He broke the connection and dialled the Paris apartment. Kirstie had not yet arrived. He left a message on the answering machine.

'Terrible news. George Drury was killed last night. I'm on my way to Maggie's. Call me there as soon as you get in.'

Her flight was due at Charles de Gaulle at nine-fifteen British time. There was an hour difference between England and France. He scraped a razor over his face, threw the wet towel at the laundry basket and pulled on jeans and a sweater. He topped these with his Hudson Bay jacket. It was ten to nine when he pulled in behind the car parked outside Maggie's house.

The doctor answered the knock on the door, wearing an overcoat over his pyjamas and slippers.

'I've been here since seven,' he explained quickly. 'I've given her an injection. It should make her sleep. There's not a lot more I can do at the moment. Are you able to stay for a while? It's important that she isn't left alone.'

Raven hung his coat on the stand in the hall. 'You mean she could harm herself?'

The doctor shrugged. His face was concerned. 'She's deeply disturbed. People in her condition sometimes do strange things. Things that are completely out of character. A friend of hers called Emma Tufnell is coming here at eleven. Do you know her?'

Raven searched his memory and nodded. She was another model who worked with Kirstie from time to time.

'Good!' The doctor produced a card. 'Here's my number in case of an emergency. Otherwise, I'll look in at six o'clock tonight.'

Raven shut the door behind him. The doctor's card bore an address in Hereford Square. Munro's practice was no more than a quarter of a mile away.

Raven climbed the stairs. The bedroom door was ajar, the curtains drawn, the reading lamp lit. Maggie was lying with her eyes shut. She opened them as he sat on the side of the bed and reached for his hand. The telephone was on the pillow next to her.

He tightened his grip on her fingers. 'Kirstie went to Paris this morning. She'll be calling here just as soon as she gets in.'

She moved her head helplessly. 'It can't be true, John,' she whispered. 'There has to be some mistake.'

'We'll talk about it later,' he soothed. Her eyes had none of their usual fire. He guessed that the sedative was taking effect. He freed his grip gently but she grabbed at him.

'You can't go!' she implored. 'Please stay with me, John!'

He rose to his feet. 'I'll be right back, Maggie. I'll make us some coffee.'

The sitting room showed signs of Maggie's long vigil. Brimming ashtrays, a half-bottle of Pernod and her address book. He brewed coffee and took the cups upstairs.

'I don't know if you're supposed to have this but drink it anyway.'

She struggled into an upright position, indifferent to her gaping pyjama jacket. She held the cup with both shaking hands.

'Don't worry,' she said. 'I'm not going to cry on you. There are no tears left.'

'You're a brave girl, Maggie,' he said with compassion. 'Do you want to talk or not?'

She put the cup down and pushed back her hair. 'I'll tell you what I know. God knows it's little enough. George had this phone-call early yesterday morning. Some American had flown in from New York and wanted to see him. That's what he said, anyway.'

Her manner gave him a clue. 'But you didn't believe him?'

She moved her head from side to side. 'He's been lying to me for a few days, John. Don't laugh, but I had this presentiment, the feeling that something dreadful was going to happen. When he didn't come home last night I was sure of it. By midnight I was frantic. I thought he might have been involved in an accident.'

'Did he take the car?' asked Raven.

'No.' A pulse in her throat beat erratically. 'I thought of calling the police but you know how he is about them. He could have walked in at any moment. He'd have raised the roof.'

'You could have called me,' he suggested.

'And said what?' She picked up the cup again. 'I was still hoping he'd come home. Drunk maybe, but home.' She looked away quickly, attempting to hide the despair in her face.

'George called me last night,' Raven said on impulse. 'He wanted a number checked. He was in a filling-station outside Dorking.'

She covered her mouth with her hand. 'But that was where the police say the accident happened, a petrol-station outside Dorking. But what was he *doing* there?'

The phone rang on the pillow beside her. She averted her face and he took the call. It was Kirstie.

'She's all right,' he said, answering his wife's opening question. 'I'm staying here until Emma Tufnell arrives at eleven. No, nobody knows what happened. We'll just have to wait.'

He spoke for another couple of minutes and hung up.

'She's catching the six o'clock flight back. She's going to spend the night with you.'

She took his hand again wearily. 'I hope you need me some day, you two.'

'That's entirely probable,' he said, searching for the right words to explain what he meant. 'I'll do whatever's necessary, Maggie. Whatever has to be done, I'll take care of it.'

She looked at him, the fullness of her eyes belying her statement that she had no tears left.

'I want you to promise me one thing, John.'

'Tell me,' said Raven.

'I want to know the truth about George. Whatever it is, I want to know it.'

'You'll know,' he assured her. He placed the empty cups on the tray and turned off the lamp beside her. 'Try to get some sleep, darling. I'll be using the phone downstairs. I'll take care of Emma when she arrives.'

He left the sitting room door open so that if she called he could hear. He sat on the sofa with the phone on his lap. His first call was to Patrick O'Callaghan but the lawyer was in court. His secretary promised that she would get a message to him. Raven dialled Chelsea Police Station. The duty sergeant told him that news of Drury's death had come from the head-quarters of Surrey County Constabulary in Guildford. Raven dialled the number the sergeant gave him. A girl on the switchboard put him through to the CID room. Raven waited while a man dealt with his enquiry. It was five minutes before he came back on the line.

'What did you say your name was, sir?'

Raven told him again and explained. 'I'm a friend of George Drury's and I'm speaking from his girlfriend's home. We're trying to get some idea of what happened.'

'You'll have to talk to the officer who's in charge of the investigation.'

'This is ridiculous,' Raven burst out. 'Look, I know some-thing about these things. This isn't a CID matter. It's a simple enquiry about an accident.'

'You'll have to talk to the officer concerned,' the man said obstinately.

Raven was losing his temper. 'Then put me on to him.'

'I'm sorry, that won't be possible. He's extremely busy at the moment.'

'What's his name?' challenged Raven.

'Detective Superintendent Capstick, but I can tell you now that he'll be busy for some time, sir.'

Raven's jawline hardened, recognising the runaround he was being given.

'Well you listen to me,' he said firmly. 'I used to be on the force myself and I know the game. A friend of mine is dead and I want to know what happened to him. If the man in charge isn't available, let me talk to someone who is.'

'I'm sorry, sir,' the voice said, stonewalling. 'We're not allowed to give this sort of information over the telephone.'

The line went dead. Raven tiptoed upstairs and took a look at Maggie. She was sleeping, breathing heavily. The doorbell rang just before eleven o'clock. A tall, dusty blonde in a tracksuit and trainers was chaining her bicycle to the lamp-post. Raven hurried her in and steered her into the sitting room.

'Hi,' she said, dropping down to the sofa. 'You're Kirstie's husband, right?'

She listened closely as he told her what had happened, smoking with nervous gestures.

'Maggie's sleeping,' he concluded. 'There are things I have to do. Kirstie should be here by eight. Can you stay until then?'

'No problem,' she said.

He gave her the doctor's card. 'He's coming by six. Let her sleep as long as she can. He's given her some sort of shot.'

'Don't worry,' she said, looking up at him. 'I know what to do. I've been through all this myself.'

The kiss she gave him was unexpected. He let himself out of the house with a new respect for her kind. Half-an-hour later he was driving along the Putney by-pass in the direction of Dorking. He found the filling-station a mile out of town. It was a desolate scene. The office and service-bay were completely burned-out, the petrol-pumps blown asunder. The foundations looked like rotting teeth stumps. Bits of timber and masonry were strewn across the ground. The telephone-box was a twisted shell. A man in rubber hip-boots was hosing the film of oil from the forecourt. Raven drove in and wound down his window.

'What happened here? he called.

The jet of water played in the air momentarily. The man's face was bleak and cold. He looked as though he had answered the same question many times.

'The place blew up is what happened,' he said.

Raven stepped from the car. Bloodstains on the ground had frozen overnight. He lit a Gitane and offered the pack to the attendant. 'It looks as though a bomb hit it,' said Raven.

'Might just as well have done.' The man took a deep drag on the cigarette and coughed violently.

Raven poked at a splinter of glass with the toe of his sneaker. 'You work here, don't you? I've seen you here before.'

The man's face was sour. 'Not any more I don't. They've given me to the end of the week to clear the place, then it's out on my ear after six years of it. Not a penny compensation. You from the newspapers?'

Raven felt in his pocket. A five-pound note changed hands.

'What *exactly* did happen?'

The man turned off the hose he was holding. 'Search me. All I know is that the law pulled me out of bed at eleven o'clock last night. They said some geezer come in here after we'd closed last night. They said he blew himself up. Lit a match or something. Seems strange to me. I mean, I never smelled no fumes.'

A twisted piece of body-trim lay on the snow-covered verge.

'Is that part of the car he was driving?' asked Raven, pointing.

The man nodded. 'Wasn't much left of it from what I hear. They'd towed it away by the time I got here.' His manner grew confidential. 'Between you and me I don't believe in no leak. We had one of them safety inspectors round only a week ago.'

Raven resumed his seat behind the steering wheel. The attendant seemed unwilling to let him go. When Raven looked up into the driving mirror the man was writing something on a piece of paper.

The headquarters of the county constabulary were reached by a drive lined with beech trees. Radio masts spiked the roof of the ugly building. Raven drew up beside a row of police vehicles and left the Saab there. He walked across to the entrance. People were coming and going in the main hallway. Office machinery clattered along the corridor. A uniformed constable detached himself from a group talking to a distressed-looking woman. The numerals on his tunic shone like silver. His face had been shaved to a point near rawness and his eyes were solemn with responsibility.

'Can I help you, sir?' he asked Raven.

'Good morning,' said Raven pleasantly. 'My name is Raven. A friend of mine was killed in an accident near Dorking last night. I'm trying to find out exactly what happened.'

'I understand, sir,' the young man said helpfully.

'Someone came round from our local police station in London,' Raven volunteered.

'And they told you to come to us?'

'No,' said Raven. 'It seemed the best place.' He smiled.

'If you'll wait a minute, sir.' The cop had a brief word with his colleagues and vanished along the corridor. He returned in a few minutes, red-faced and clearly embarrassed. The man with him was grey-haired, with dark, hostile eyes and wearing a sports jacket with leather patches on the elbows. The constable led him to Raven.

'This is the gentleman, sir,' the young policeman said stiffly.

The other man nodded without offering his hand. 'Detective Superintendent Capstick. Come with me, please.' He led the way along the corridor and opened a door.

Raven knew the scene well, the interview rooms for people who were viewed with suspicion but against whom there was no evidence as yet. There were a deal table and two plain chairs. The walls were painted a drab shade of olive. Dead flies were trapped in the space between the double-glazed windows, and the linoleum was badly scuffed. It was a room to which few would come by choice.

Capstick closed the door. 'Are you the person who phoned earlier today, spoke to one of my officers?'

'That's me,' said Raven. He reached for a cigarette.

'No smoking in here,' Capstick said firmly. 'Are you a journalist, Mr Raven?'

'I'm not, no,' answered Raven. He had the impression that his visit to the filling-station was already known. 'What makes you ask?'

'It's part of my job,' said the detective. 'You could be

anyone. We have a duty to the bereaved family in a situation like this.

'There *is* no bereaved family,' Raven replied. 'All George had was his friends and the woman he shared his life with. I'm one of the friends.'

Capstick glanced through the dusty windows. A couple of police cars had been moved outside, leaving Raven's Saab prominent in the car park.

'I understand you've been asking questions at the Dominion Petrol Station,' said Capstick.

'I was there,' Raven admitted. He extracted his expired Metropolitan Police Force warrant-card. 'I was with the Met for seventeen years and I do know the score, Superintendent.'

'I'm sure of that,' said the officer. He took a close look at the warrant-card before returning it. 'What do you do now? What's your occupation?'

Tension was building between the two men and Raven was aware of it.

'I do nothing,' he said.

Capstick lifted an accusing finger. 'You know you've got a very aggressive attitude, Mr Raven. I expect you've been told that before.'

'Frequently,' said Raven. 'It helps when you're dealing with obstinate people. In fact it's often the only way. I'm no ghoul, Superintendent. It so happens that I've just left a woman lying in bed stuffed full of tranquillisers. She's lost the man she's been living with for the past five years and she'd like to know what happened to him. *I'd* like to know what happened to him.'

The detective widened his stance. 'We've already been in touch with Mr Drury's legal representative.'

'Patrick O'Callaghan,' Raven said quickly. 'He's a friend of mine too and my lawyer.'

The policeman's smile was humourless. 'Then my advice is to contact him. He has all the relevant information.'

'When's the inquest?' Raven demanded.

'That's up to the coroner. His office will be in touch with Mr O'Callaghan.' Capstick made a point of consulting his watch.

Raven had no thought of giving up yet. 'Do you know who signed the death certificate?'

'No I do not,' Capstick said heavily. 'I don't even know if there *is* a death certificate.'

'There has to be one,' insisted Raven. 'Otherwise there can't be a funeral.'

Capstick stared through the window again.

'This *is* an accident, isn't it?' Raven said suddenly.

The detective swung round. 'I've told you all I can. This is a matter that's still *sub judice*!'

'You've got a nice touch with the Latin,' Raven said sarcastically. 'Thanks.'

Capstick opened the door to the corridor. The fresh-faced youngster was waiting outside.

'See Mr Raven off the premises,' Capstick said curtly.

The constable accompanied Raven outside. Someone had stuck a notice on the windscreen of the Saab.

**THIS SPACE IS RESERVED FOR OFFICIAL VEHICLES!
FAILURE TO OBSERVE THIS REGULATION IN
FUTURE WILL RESULT IN THE REMOVAL OF YOUR
CAR
YOU HAVE BEEN WARNED!**

The constable was clearly embarrassed. 'I'm afraid that was me. I was told to do it.'

Raven deposited the sticker in a dustbin. He climbed behind the wheel of the Saab and wound down the window.

'Let me tell you something about being a cop,' he said to the constable. 'If you manage to be a good one it'll be in spite of the people you work with. Remember that!'

Capstick was at a second-floor window. The youngster's voice was hardly audible.

'Try the hospital.'

Raven let in the clutch.

The hospital was built on a hill overlooking the university. It was a complex of modern buildings connected by underpasses with landscaped grounds. Guildford Central looked what it was, a well-equipped medical centre funded by a wealthy county. Raven found the main entrance. Inside there was an air of brisk efficiency. Nurses had walkie-talkies clipped to their tunics. Electrically assisted stretchers glided by. Raven followed the signs to the reception area. A girl in white nylon glanced up from her desk.

'May I help you?'

Raven smiled winningly. 'I'm called John Raven. Good morning. I'm trying to find out what happened to someone called George Drury. He was killed in an accident near Dorking last night and I understand the body was brought here.'

She scribbled on a pad and gestured to a nearby bench. 'If you'll take a seat I'll get someone to deal with you.'

He watched her from the bench as she used the telephone. It was some time before a man emerged from the elevator. He was a neatly dressed individual carrying with him an air of intimidating authority. His pale hair was thin and he had what appeared to be a third eyebrow pasted across his upper lip. He strode across the reception area.

'Mr Raven? My name is Hoogstraten. I'm the Hospital Administrator. I understand you're making enquiries about an accident that took place last night.'

Raven came to his feet, topping Hoogstraten by four inches.

'That's right. The man was a friend of mine. George Drury. All we know is that he's dead. I'm trying to find out what happened.'

Hoogstraten sat down on the bench, holding a piece of paper in his hand. He had the smooth manner of someone skilled in fending off awkward questions.

'Of course,' he said quickly. 'It's entirely natural. This is a copy of the ambulance log. The call for assistance came from the Dorking police at nine forty-seven last night. The ambulance reached the scene fifteen minutes later. I'm afraid the victim was found to be dead on arrival. The remains were removed to the mortuary just before midnight. I hope that's of help.' He pocketed the piece of paper and smiled perfunctorily.

'It doesn't help a lot, no,' answered Raven. It struck him as odd that the man had chosen to deal with the enquiry personally.

'It doesn't tell me what happened to my friend. There's talk about an accident, an explosion of some kind, but nobody seems to have details. Is it possible for me to talk to the doctor who signed the death certificate.

Hoogstraten shook his head. A current of understanding seemed to flow between him and the nurse behind the reception desk.

'I'm afraid not,' he said. 'The doctor concerned is on leave.'

'Since when?' Raven asked.

'Since this morning.' Hoogstraten's manner was bland. 'I'm afraid I can't do any more for you.'

Both men rose. Raven was insistent. 'I'd have thought the doctor would have to attend the inquest.'

'I'm sure he will,' said Hoogstraten. 'Now if you'll excuse me.'

Raven continued to block his way. 'A man has been killed in an accident. The police don't want to talk about it nor do you. Why?'

Hoogstraten stepped round him smartly and made for the elevator. The receptionist busied herself with some papers. Raven left the building, angry and frustrated. He sat in the car, staring across the vast car park.

Why were they trying to hush this thing up? Could it be some freak mishap the authorities needed to keep quiet? Exploration of the idea left too many questions unanswered. One thing was certain. George had been alive at ten minutes to nine. Only the inquest would explain what came later.

Raven stopped at a pub a few miles out of Guildford. It was a typical roadside hostelry with fake beams and fast food. He carried his beer and sandwich to a seat near the telephone and called Patrick O'Callaghan.

'I got your message,' said the lawyer. 'I tried to reach you at

Maggie's but you'd already left. Where are you now?'

'I'm on my way back from Guildford. I've been seeing the police and the hospital people. There's something going on that I don't understand, Patrick. When can I see you?'

There was a pause as the lawyer consulted his secretary.

'I can't move until five,' he said. 'Shall I come to the boat or what?'

'I'll see you then,' said Raven.

The sky was dark with the threat of more snow when Raven reached London. He parked in the dead-end opposite the boat and went down the steps to the gangplank door. The *Albatross* wallowed like a whale on the incoming tide. A few ducks were cruising through the green-topped backwater. He let himself into the sitting room and felt for the switch. A picture lamp lit the Paul Klee painting. Kirstie loathed it but Raven found comfort in the Swiss artist's sense of form and colour. Emma Tufnell answered his call. Maggie had drunk some soup and had gone back to sleep. Kirstie had phoned from Paris confirming her arrival time. Raven walked through to the kitchen and removed his shoes. His mind was still with Drury. It was difficult to accept his friend's death. The redheaded Cockney had carried an aura of permanence. Raven retraced his steps over the past hours and got nowhere.

The doorbell rang at ten past five. Raven buzzed the entry, releasing the catch on the door. O'Callaghan hurried along the deck. Raven let him in. The lawyer's nose was pink from the cold. He was a slim man, dapper in a chalk-striped business suit and bold tweed overcoat. He had a narrow moustache, wayward hair and a bow-tie he wore askew.

He bounced on the sofa, nodding at the drinks cupboard.

'A Scotch, please. I tell you, I need one.'

Raven fixed two. The lawyer drank his quickly and held out his glass for a refill.

'OK,' he said, 'you go first!'

Raven drew the curtains and told him what had happened.

'I'm not sure what it is,' he concluded, 'but there's something very dodgy going on.'

O'Callaghan held his cigarette like a pen, between thumb and forefinger.

'I had a call from the Guildford coroner's office half-an-hour ago.'

'Well at least we're getting somewhere,' said Raven. 'When's it going to be?'

'They can't say. Or won't. But the inquest's going to be held *in camera*.'

'*In camera*?' Raven repeated. 'What the hell's that supposed to mean?'

The words slid easily from the lawyer's lips. 'It means that it'll be closed to the public. Maggie won't be allowed to attend. You won't be allowed to attend. I'm not even sure that I will.'

Raven shook his head in disbelief. 'But how can they do that, Patrick?'

O'Callaghan shrugged his slender shoulders. 'The Official Secrets Act.'

'The Official Secrets Act! I have to be losing my mind! We're talking about a second-hand car dealer who blew himself up!'

'I know that as well as you do.' The lawyer dribbled smoke from his nostrils. 'They can certainly bar the public and press but as I say I'm not sure about me. I'm taking counsel's opinion tomorrow morning.'

Raven poured himself another Scotch. 'And is that what I'm supposed to tell Maggie?'

'I don't know what you're going to tell Maggie,' the lawyer answered. 'But we'd better tell the same story. The order comes from the Home Office. That's what the coroner's office says. "The evidence may touch upon sensitive areas dealing with national security."'

Raven hit his forehead with the heel of his hand. '*National security*! What the hell can George have had to do with national security? What are they trying to say, that he was some sort of a spy?'

'You're still asking the hard questions.' The lawyer extinguished his cigarette with a cat-like movement employing the least amount of energy necessary. 'Once the inquest's over they'll release the body for burial. Someone will have to deal with the funeral arrangements.'

Raven took a turn to his desk and back, adjusting to the swaying of the boat.

'Maggie's in no condition to talk about funerals. We'll have to take care of it. Do you know what I think, Patrick? I think this is all some kind of conspiracy. OK, George calls me from the filling-station just before nine o'clock, wanting me to check a house near Horsham. I do that and there's no reply. Half-an-hour later he's dead.'

O'Callaghan's eyes were curious. 'Did you tell the police about that?'

'No, said Raven. 'You're the first person I've told.'

The two men looked at one another speculatively. Raven spoke on impulse.

'Did you know about George's tax problems?'

'Of course,' said the lawyer. 'George always had tax problems.'

'Nearly twenty-eight thousand pounds' worth?' Raven challenged. 'And the bill was paid in full a couple of days ago! Where would George get that sort of money?'

'Maggie?' the lawyer suggested.

'No,' said Raven. 'And that's the only place he could have borrowed it. What would he use as collateral? A collection of clapped-out motor-cars and a lease on half an acre of cinders in South London?'

'The Americans?' O'Callaghan ventured. 'The people he saw in New York. The ones with the franchise to sell cars in Europe to American servicemen.'

'Without getting you to look at the contract? Without saying a word to anyone close to him? Bullshit, Patrick. Do you want to know what I think?'

O'Callaghan showed small, sharp teeth. 'Whatever it is, I've got a feeling that I won't like it.'

'I think George was killed – murdered.' Raven said quietly.

O'Callaghan cast his eyes in despair. 'You know, Kirstie's right! Everything has to be seen in terms of high drama as far as you're concerned.'

'And how do *you* see it?' Raven objected. 'A friend of yours, and a client, gets blown asunder. The police say it was an accident but they won't talk about it. The hospital doesn't want to know and the inquest's going to be held *in camera*. What does all this add up to in *your* book?'

'You're being ridiculous,' said the lawyer. 'If the police even suspected murder you'd still be in Guildford Police Station. They'd be all over you.'

'Would they?' Raven asked politely. 'How about if *they* were part of the conspiracy? And this business about the Official Secrets Act. What's your view on that?'

The lawyer's stare was steady. 'I don't have a view, at least not yet. I don't share your vivid imagination. There isn't a shred of evidence to back up your claims.'

'There's this,' Raven said, tapping the side of his nose. 'And it's one of the best in the business.'

O'Callaghan stretched out his legs. 'It seems to me that I've heard all this before, not once but many, many times.'

'And have I been right?'

'Most of the time you've been wrong, looking at things from a rational point of view.'

'Bullshit,' said Raven. 'Results are what matter. I believe George was killed. I believe the authorities know he was killed and I think they're doing a snow job on the whole thing.'

The enormity of what he was saying drew both men into a silence that was finally broken by the lawyer.

'This is something that I've got to say to you, John. OK, you get results, but you drag others in with you. People who don't have your flair for dealing in danger.'

The fact that what his friend said was true made it no less unpalatable to Raven.

'Think about it,' the lawyer said quietly. 'Who would want to kill George and why? I'm talking about the sort of people with enough clout to invoke the Official Secrets Act. If you can't answer that I'm going to wait for the authorised version. Even if I'm not allowed into the inquest I'll get a copy of the transcript.'

Raven knew the other man well. And right now the lawyer was digging his heels in. Raven balled his shoulders. 'OK, I'll tell you what I'm going to do. I'm going down to that house that George wanted checked. I've looked it up in the reference books. It's called Capel Manor and belongs to someone called Hansen. According to the electoral list there are three people living there, Hansen and a married couple. The telephone number is ex-directory. I keep calling it but nobody answers.'

The lawyer looked at him. 'Suddenly this isn't funny any more, John. I can't stop you going off half-cocked. I never have been able to.'

'You're missing the point,' argued Raven. 'Are you going to help me or not?'

The lawyer raised a hand in submission. 'I suppose it's my duty to keep you out of prison.'

Raven grinned, excited by the prospect of the hunt. 'No one else has to know about this,' he warned. 'No one must know what I'm doing.'

'They will,' said the lawyer. 'You'll take good care of that. Anyway I have to go.' He looked through the curtains and shivered.

Raven held the lawyer's overcoat for him. 'Are you coming round to Maggie's later?'

'I can't,' said the lawyer. 'I have to go back to the office.'

'Maggie's sure to ask if I have seen you.' Raven knew his friend's uneasiness at any form of emotional display.

'Tell her whatever you think is right,' said the lawyer, buttoning up his overcoat. 'I'm doing duty-solicitor at Horseferry Road tomorrow morning but I'll be back in the office after lunch. Call me there and let me know what's happening.' He thought for a moment and added. 'Be careful, John.'

Raven waited on deck until the lawyer's footsteps were no longer heard. Alone again, he thought of what he must do. He went to his bookshelves and drew out Stacey's *Sussex Manor-houses* and the *Directory of Directors*. Capel Manor was the subject of half a page. A coloured plate showed an elegant redbrick house surrounded by trees and water. He opened the other book. An entry gave the name Hansen p.l.c., 240 Saint James's Street, London SW1. The company secretary was given as Harold Garrison, Solicitor, of the same address. No other details were supplied. Raven opened a road atlas and found Warnham in an angle between the main Chichester and Eastbourne roads. He returned the books to their places and went into the kitchen. One of Mrs Burrows' fish pies from the freezer took only minutes to heat in the micro-wave. The meal over, he washed his dirty plate and considered what to tell his wife. He decided to stall for as long as he could. It wasn't a question of Kirstie's allegiance to her friends. That was total. What worried her was Raven's way of coming to their aid.

He was at Cresswell Place shortly after eight o'clock. Kirstie opened the door. He held her tight, letting her go only when she gasped for breath. He followed her into the sitting room. Her flight-bag was on a chair.

'Emma only just went,' she informed him. 'I got a cab from Heathrow.'

She had changed her clothes in Paris. He recognised the black velvet suit.

'How's Maggie?' he asked.

She pushed a handful of whisky-coloured hair behind an ear.

'She's sleeping. Emma said the doctor came by earlier than expected and gave her another shot. What exactly happened with George, darling? Nobody really seems to know anything.'

She rarely wept, but he could see that she was close to it. He pulled her down on the sofa beside him.

'You're right about nobody knowing,' he said. 'And that includes the police. The accident happened down in the country, just outside Dorking. An explosion outside a service-station, they say. They're waiting for forensic tests to be made.' There was no real lie in what he said, but he was glad it was out.

She sprang to her feet suddenly. 'I need a drink. Can I get you one?'

He shook his head. 'I had a couple on the boat with Patrick.'

She half-filled a glass with Dubonnet and added ice.

'Poor Maggie,' she said. 'What are we going to do with her, darling? I feel so *helpless*.'

'What we have to do is stay close to her,' he answered. 'The doctor says she shouldn't be left alone.'

'She won't,' Kirstie said with assurance. 'Either I stay here or she comes to us.'

He spread his hands. 'Whatever you feel. She'd probably prefer to stay here.'

Her eyes came alive with sudden anxiety. 'But what about you? Will you be all right on your own?'

'I'll survive, he said soberly. 'After all, I'll have Mrs Burrows to take care of me.' A guarded but deep dislike existed between his wife and cleaning lady.

'I'll bet,' said Kirstie drily. 'I can read you like a book, my friend. You'll be delighted to be on your own.'

'Best way to preserve a romance,' he said. 'Separate establishments.'

He liked to light the occasional fire under her.

Her expression softened. 'Shall I make you something to eat?'

'I ate on the boat,' he said. 'You look tired. Why don't you lie down and rest? There's nothing you can do for Maggie except be here.'

She cocked her head. 'You wouldn't mind? I'm not behaving in a very wifely manner.'

He took her face in his hands and kissed her lips. 'I'm going anyway,' he said. 'And you're doing just fine. Come to think of it, I'm glad I married you.'

Her gaze lingered on his face. 'You never belonged to anyone else, John Raven. *Never!*'

'Call me in the morning,' he said. 'Let me know what you and Maggie decide to do. Try to put her mind at rest about the funeral. Patrick and I will take care of it.'

She came to the hall with him. Then the front door closed.

* * *

91

Morning broke with the same wintry desolation. An east wind was cracking the flag flying from the stern of the houseboat. Raven had dressed and was eating his breakfast when Kirstie called.

'Maggie's decided to stay here,' she announced. 'Emma and I are going to take shifts for the moment. I'll be coming home later to pick up some things. What are your plans?'

'I have to go down to the country,' he said. Stacey on *Sussex Manorhouses* lay open on the table in front of him next to his camera. 'I'll come over tonight, OK?'

He emptied the mailbox and collected his newspapers. He glanced through them, sitting in the Saab while the motor warmed up. There was no mention at all of George Drury's death, no reference to the petrol-station or an explosion.

The roads had been gritted and he made good time down to Warnham. Signs directed him along meandering lanes to a village green where children had built a coal-eyed snowman. A bell tinkled as Raven opened the door to the grocery store. There was a smell of cheese, spices and kerosene. The woman behind the counter wore her hair in an old-fashioned bun skewered with a pencil.

'I'm looking for Capel Manor,' he explained.

'Are you walking or driving?' she asked.

'Driving.' He was pretty sure that she'd seen his arrival.

A man appeared from the inner room. 'Gentleman's looking for the manor,' she said.

The man lifted a flap in the counter, walked to the door and inspected the Saab outside. He had the beady eyes and pursed mouth of the village busybody.

'Well you'll have to turn round for a start,' he said. 'Then you go past the green and left at the riding stable. You'll see the manor half-a-mile on, opposite the water-tower. From London are you, a friend of Mr Hansen's?'

Raven just smiled at him. The instructions led him down a high-hedged lane to the Dene Riding Centre. Children were trotting ponies round a snow-covered paddock. The road dipped suddenly, picking up a wall on the left. A five-barred gate was shut at the top of the drive. Raven slowed. The curve of tarmac vanished through a plantation of Scots pines and beeches. He continued along the lane which ran parallel with the brick wall. After half-a-mile the wall turned away at a right-angle, marking the boundary of the property. A rough track through the trees accompanied it.

Raven turned on to the track, stopping the Saab once he was out of sight of the lane. He took the Pentax from the glove compartment and stuffed the book in his lumberjacket pocket. The camera was loaded with film. He locked the car and started to walk. The wall was a dozen feet high. Overhanging branches had been trimmed from the trees near the track making it difficult for anyone to use them to scale the wall. A couple of hundred yards on he found a door in the wall, partially concealed by ivy. Close inspection showed that the lock was clogged with ancient dirt. Patently it had not been used for some time. He took a suede roll from his pocket. The tools inside were a present from a burglar Raven had put away. The second skeleton key Raven tried turned the lock, but the door held fast. He inserted a pick between door and jamb and found that a bolt had been pushed home on the other side. He put the tools away, stepped back eyeing the wall and then ran. He rose in the air, hanging briefly like a basketball player, scrambled over the top of the wall and dropped. He picked himself up gingerly, convinced that something had been broken. He was wrong.

A rook cawed from a point of vantage. A beating of wings announced the departure of others. He walked towards the dank smell of water, the Pentax in hand. The trees gave way to rhododendrons and azaleas. Rushes fringed a gelid lake. He was standing in front of a weathered redbrick house with white-framed windows. The ground-floor windows were shuttered. He crossed the gravelled turning-circle, aiming the camera haphazardly. The garden was cared for, the bushes trimmed. The tips of spring bulbs peeped through the snow.

Raven put his thumb on the bell-push and heard it ring somewhere at the back of the house. There was no response. A second ring was no more successful. He stepped back, looking up at the second-floor windows. He cupped his hands and called. The sound echoed in the trees and vanished. An archway led to a large, cobbled yard with a metal garage door on the left. The kitchen was on the opposite side of the yard. He raised the garage door. Inside was a Rolls-Royce Corniche. Its paintwork bore the patina of constant attention. He touched the radiator with his hand. It was cold. He dropped the door again and peered through the kitchen window.

An earthenware bowl filled with daffodils stood on the table. Everything looked clean and in place. The kitchen door had been locked on the inside, the key left in position, the tips protruding outside. Raven selected a pair of longnosed forceps from his burglary kit and clamped them over the tip. The key turned with the movement of his wrist. The door opened easily. He locked it again and tiptoed across the kitchen to a green baize door. Beyond that was darkness. A clock was ticking sonorously close at hand. He felt for a light-switch. Candlesticks held by gilded figures illuminated the hall. The grandfather clock stood at the foot of the staircase. He glanced down at the parquet floor. A dull patch in the polish denoted the size of the rug that had lain there. An attempt had been made to erase the stains in the boards but he knew what they were. He had a sudden feeling that George Drury had stood in this hall.

He turned the handle of the door in front of him. Enough light came through the drawn curtains to make out the heavy furniture, the dead ashes in the fireplace. He climbed the stairs. Light streamed along the corridors. He opened one cream-coloured door after another until he came to the master bedroom. The brocade walls were hung with Japanese erotic prints. A low bed stood between revolving bookcases. Raven explored the enormous Breton wardrobe. Tailors' labels in the clothes hanging inside bore the name Sven Hansen. He found an envelope with a Swiss stamp in a jacket pocket. It was addressed to Sven Hansen and dated the previous month. He read the letter inside.

c/o Bierkelback & Unkrauer
Bärengasse
ZÜRICH Switzerland

Dear Sven,

As I told you on the phone, I managed to put the Armalite deal together. The price is as agreed, one million three hundred thousand dollars ($1,300,000). This price will include two million rounds of ammunition. There *must* be a Final Destination Certificate and the Ministry of Trade permit. I strongly urge acceptance of these terms and will send the contract.

All best

Joe.

He put the letter back in the jacket and closed the armoire. Tyres sounded on the gravel below. He hurried across the corridor and flattened himself against the wall, peeping down through the curtains. A black Cadillac had drawn up in front of the entrance. The driver emerged, stretching his arms as he glanced around. He looked to be in his late twenties, well dressed in the Madison Avenue image and wearing a snapbrim hat. Raven heard the front door being opened. He undid the window-catch and readied himself to drop to the ground and start running. Silence shifted as he waited. Then the house was quiet again. The man had gone through the hall and out by the back door.

Raven ran lightly down the stairs. A new rug covered the stain in the hallway. Raven let himself out with infinite care. The house allowed him to leave without quibble. He wiped his neck, adjusted the heavy jacket and headed up the driveway with a lively sense of urgency. There was no sound of pursuit as he trotted past the rushes by the lake. He swung round on impulse, aiming the Pentax at the front of the house. As he reached the next bend in the drive, the man from the Cadillac stepped from the trees. He moved in front of Raven, blocking his passage. The Beretta he was holding was aimed at Raven's belly. His accent was American.

'Looking for somebody?'

Raven raised the camera on its braided sling. 'Just taking some pictures.'

The man moved a couple of steps closer, polite but hard-eyed. 'Don't you know that you're on private property?'

'I'm sorry,' said Raven. 'I did ring the bell at the house but there was no answer.'

'Give me the camera!' The American held out his hand.

Raven surrendered it. The man unfastened the chassis and ripped out the film. 'Here,' he said, returning the camera. 'Which paper are you with?' he asked.

'You're making a mistake,' said Raven, shaking his head. 'I'm not a reporter. I just happen to like period houses. Other people take pictures of women. I take pictures of houses.' To his own ears the speech sounded totally false.

'I think you're full of shit,' the American said in a flat, even voice. The gun was still trained on Raven's stomach. 'Let's see some identification.'

'Hang on a minute,' Raven objected. 'You can't go around pulling guns on people!'

'Identification!' the man said, snapping his fingers. 'We can call the police if you'd rather have that.'

Something in the man's tone warned Raven to do as he said.

'OK, put the gun away.'

The man unbuttoned his jacket and pushed the Beretta into his waistband. 'What were you running for?'

'I was jogging,' said Raven. 'It's cold. I couldn't run twenty yards.' He pulled up his trouser-leg and displayed his varicose vein scars.

The American leafed through the contents of Raven's wallet, inspecting driving licence, credit-cards and insurance policies. His expression changed as he came to the out-of-date warrant-card. His tone was surprised.

'This is you?'

'It was,' answered Raven. 'I resigned some years ago. I carry it to impress people.'

The American pulled the gun from his belt and ran his free

hand over Raven's body. He stiffened visibly as his hand touched the bulge in the lumberjacket. His fingers closed on it.

'What's this?' he said suspiciously.

Raven pulled the book out. He opened it at a marked page.

'I called the house this morning for permission to take some photographs. Nobody answered.'

The American's eyes were stony. 'The number's ex-directory.'

Raven shifted his weight from one leg to the other. 'I know how to get it.'

'I'm sure you do,' the other man said sarcastically. 'Let's go over it again, shall we? You woke up this morning with nothing else in the wide world to do except drive down here and take pictures of somebody else's house, right?'

'Right,' said Raven. 'You can make anything sound stupid putting it that way.'

'How did you get here?'

'I drove. My car's some way along. I pulled off the road because it's so narrow.'

The man discontinued his body-search after finding the book. His next move would have taken him to Raven's hip pocket and the roll of burglar tools. His eyes sought Raven's face.

'You must have heard me arrive. Why didn't you show yourself?'

'I've already tried to explain. I got here and rang the bell. Nobody answered so I took some pictures at the back of the house. I was over by the lake when I heard the car coming. I still couldn't see anybody. End of story.'

The American appeared to make up his mind. He returned Raven's wallet. 'I want you off this property fast,' he said. 'Take a hike through that gate and keep going.'

Raven retreated, feeling as though he had just been struck by a flying anvil. He managed to walk like a man with no problems, conscious that he was still being watched. The gate at the end of the driveway was open. He hurried along the lane to the parked Saab, turned the ignition-key and heard the sweet hum of the motor. He drove back to London making frequent references to the rear-view mirror. It was after six o'clock when he turned into Upper Berkeley Street. Patrick O'Callaghan's offices were on the second floor. Raven turned the door-handle. The outer office was empty, dust-covers spread over the word processor and telex machine. Raven tapped and entered his friend's room. O'Callaghan's desk was littered with correspondence and theatre programmes. Photographs of his parents hung on the wall, a morning-suit on the back of the door. Pink-taped briefs had been stuffed into laundry baskets.

Raven cleared a chair. The lawyer looked at him. 'Who knows what evil lurks in the hearts of men?' he intoned. 'Only the Shadow knows.'

'Hilarious,' Raven said drily. 'Is that it or is there more? I don't have much time.'

O'Callaghan's smile faded. 'That's a bad sign. You're losing your sense of humour.'

'How could I?' Raven reported. 'The people I mix with. I want to ask you a serious question, Patrick. Do you think the American secret service operates in this country?'

The lawyer's response was swift. 'I know it does. I mean there've been books. People who were in the CIA. The whole thing given, chapter and verse, complete with names, addresses and photographs.'

'I think the CIA or someone like them are involved in George's death.' Raven allowed time for it to sink in.

O'Callaghan ran a thumbnail left and right along his moustache.

'Are you being serious?'

Raven nodded. 'Let me tell you what happened to me this afternoon.' It took him ten minutes.

'Question number one,' the lawyer said when Raven had finished. 'How do you know that it was blood that you saw in the house?'

That was easily fielded. 'Because knowing the difference from blood and ketchup used to be part of my business. I can give you details if you like, but they're not particularly attractive.'

'And you say there were no signs of anyone living there?'

'Of course there were signs! There was a Rolls Royce in the garage, food in the kitchen, clothes upstairs in the bedroom. But the only person I saw was the man who stopped me outside.'

The lawyer shifted the lamp on his desk so that the light no longer shone in their eyes.

'The blood – if it was blood – can hardly have been George's.'

'I'm not suggesting it was,' countered Raven. 'What I'm saying is that a body had been in that hall and George knew about it.'

O'Callaghan placed the tips of his fingers together. 'And the body was removed?'

'Why not,' challenged Raven. 'Do you find that far-fetched? If these people are who I think they are, then they're special.'

'Did the man who stopped you tell you his name?'

'He didn't have to,' said Raven. 'He was a good fifteen years younger than I was and he had a gun in his hand. A nine millimetre Beretta to be precise. They're deadly. On top of that I was trespassing on someone else's property with burglary tools in my pocket. I was in no position to ask him what his name was.'

'What about the Mafia?' the lawyer suggested. 'It's the sort of thing that George might well be mixed up in.'

'No chance!' Raven spoke with total assurance. 'This man was a different class.'

His friend's expression was tinged with disappointment. 'So what do you propose to do now?'

The chair creaked as Raven leaned back. 'I don't know,' he admitted after a while. 'But there's one thing I do know. I'm not letting this thing go.'

The lawyer passed his fingertips across his forehead. 'Suppose you are right,' he said. 'Suppose people like the CIA *are* involved. It would have to be with the approval of the authorities here.'

'So?' said Raven. 'I'm saying not only with their approval but with their help.'

O'Callaghan changed the subject suddenly. 'The inquest was held this afternoon.'

It was seconds before Raven registered what the other had said. Even then he found it hard to believe.

'You mean you've been sitting here for twenty minutes without telling me?' he burst out.

The lawyer raised his shoulders. 'I didn't have much opportunity. The Coroner's Office phoned through just after six. The verdict was "Death by Misadventure", cause of death "Multiple injuries resulting from an explosion".'

'But I thought you were supposed to be there?' Raven objected.

O'Callaghan shook his head. 'Counsel's opinion was negative.'

'That does it,' said Raven. His chair came down with a thud.

'Don't you see what we're up against? This is the bloody Establishment, Patrick!'

The lawyer agreed with reluctance. 'It certainly looks that way. Logic is against it but there you are. The thing now is what do we tell Maggie – or for that matter, Kirstie?'

Raven gave it some thought. 'I suppose this means that the body's released for burial?'

O'Callaghan nodded and rummaged through the papers in front of him until he found an address and telephone number.

'I've been on to the undertakers. There's not a lot they can do until we find out what Maggie wants.' He shook his head again. 'I still find it hard to believe that he's dead.'

'I intend to know *how* he died,' Raven said firmly. 'I used to get paid for this kind of thing. Now there are personal reasons.'

'And Kirstie? What are you going to tell her?'

'I'm not sure,' said Raven.

'She'll be your big problem,' the lawyer warned. 'It's all right while she has Maggie to worry about, but if this thing goes on for any length of time she's bound to rumble. She knows you too well.'

'I'll worry about that when and if,' said Raven. 'In the meantime I'm relying on you for advice and assistance.'

The lawyer came to his feet behind the desk. 'That goes without saying. I'd rather know what you're doing than not. That way at least I'm prepared. Incidentally I called George's bank this afternoon. I'm his executor. The money that paid his tax bill was telexed from Curaçao.'

Raven made a face. 'That doesn't get us far. Will you be here for a while?'

The lawyer nodded at the pile of correspondence on his desk.

'For an hour at least. Once summer's here I'll start getting up at six in the morning again. It's amazing how much work you get done between six and seven. You take your phone off the hook, of course.'

'That's what I wanted to talk to you about,' said Raven. 'If I don't call back within the hour your line will be tapped. Be careful what you say on the phone.'

O'Callaghan's eyes widened. 'You're joking, of course!'

'I'm not joking,' said Raven. 'You're George's lawyer, aren't you? I'll talk to you later, one way or another.'

He raised a hand and left. He drove south across Wandsworth Bridge and parked near the Dogs' Home. The café was a hundred yards away. The atmosphere behind the steamed windows was thick with cigarette smoke and the greasy fumes of frying bacon. Workers from a nearby building site occupied most of the tables. The man Raven was meeting was sitting by himself at the counter. Raven took the seat next to him. He ordered a cup of tea. The two men eyed one another in the mirror facing them.

The Telecom engineer spoke without turning his head.

'Your number's clean. So are the other two.'

'Are you sure?' asked Raven. 'It's important.'

'Certain,' the man said. 'The instructions come through us if they're from the police or the Home Office.'

His hand closed on the twenty-pound note Raven placed on the counter. He vanished into the street. Raven followed after a couple of minutes, leaving the stewed tea untouched. He was no more than partially reassured. The security forces use more sophisticated apparatus for their taps, equipment that registered impulses by induction and which had no direct contact with the telephone cables. There was nothing he could do about that except exercise caution.

He called the lawyer from a nearby phone box. 'Both your numbers are clean,' he said, 'home and office. 'Just be prudent.'

'I was thinking about that,' said O'Callaghan. 'A lawyer's telephone calls are privileged.'

'Try telling that to the man who stopped me this afternoon,' Raven said. 'I'll be in touch.'

Back on the boat, he sat in the darkened sitting room, staring across the river. He was suddenly glad that Kirstie was at Maggie's.

9

Kiegel stood in front of the looking-glass, inspecting the nick on his Adam's apple.

'Where's Battaglia as of this moment?'

Loovey turned from the French-windows. The two men were in the Hurlingham house; Kiegel had landed an hour before.

'I guess he'd be planted by now,' said Loovey. 'I'd have thought you'd know that. I sent a signal to Fentiman.'

Kiegel swung round. The electric razor had left his throat raw. 'I haven't talked with Fentiman. New York pulled me out of bed. The State Department's stomping on Fentiman. That's why I'm here. He wants to know what's going on.'

'What's going on is the way it was written. Joe's gone. Forever. We flew him back in a Convair. He's supposed to be buried in Tampa, name of Paesano on the headstone. What *is* this shit, Ken? Fentiman's supposed to know all this.'

Kiegel's manner was confidential. 'He's under pressure, Phil. And he doesn't trust signals. "Word of mouth," he keeps saying. All he wants now is the Battaglia file to go away.'

'Fuck him,' Loovey said calmly. 'What's he think, he's the only one in tune? We've done a good job here.'

Kiegel glanced round the room with distaste. A half-eaten sandwich was on a plate on the floor with an empty Coke can.

'These guys are animals,' he said.

Loovey understood. He was being reminded that Shaky Jake and Stepka were his protégés.

'You don't pick them for their social graces,' he answered.

Kiegel found it hard to remove his gaze from the things that offended him.

'The sooner you get them home the better. We don't want

this type of individual running around loose over here.'

Loovey jerked his head in assent. In a sense Kiegel was his mentor, but he was sick of Kiegel and sick of the conversation.

'I booked you into the Savoy,' he said, trying to change the subject. 'A room at the back; you'll be quiet.'

Kiegel stifled a yawn with his palm. 'What's all this about Hansen? Fentiman couldn't make it out.'

'Hansen's all right,' said Loovey. 'Don't even think about him. He's holed up somewhere with that broad of his, praying to God that Joe's really dead. Joe was never a man to fink on.' His smile indicated that the remark was supposed to be humorous.

Kiegel's stare was unmoved. 'Then what the hell has gone wrong, Phil?'

Loovey supplied the information unwillingly. 'I found someone wandering about the grounds of Hansen's house with a camera.'

'Holy shit!' Kiegel wiped the corners of his eyes with a handkerchief. 'Who was he?'

'A guy called Raven. I thought he was a reporter. I destroyed the film in his camera. He turned out to be an ex-cop. He had a card in his wallet to prove it.'

Kiegel winced. 'Jesus God! Does Fentiman know about this?'

'No,' Loovey said coolly. 'There's no need for him to know. There's no problem, everything's been taken care of.'

'I hope you're right, for your sake,' said Kiegel.

'Not you!' Loovey grinned like a cornered wolf. 'They get my arse, you'll be delighted.'

Kiegel looked at him curiously. 'You know you've got a weird head, Phil. Without me you wouldn't even be here.'

'Sure. You wanted to see me fall flat on my face.'

Kiegel threw up a hand. 'You've a warped sense of humour. There's something else. You overbid your hand with Drury. That was messy. He was supposed to live on.'

'I never overbid,' said Loovey. His confidence was coming back again. 'The guy knew too much.'

'It's the way it was done,' Kiegel objected. 'Whose idea was that?'

'Mine,' admitted Loovey. 'The spade's an explosives expert and a good one. Nothing was left of the car. They don't even know what make it was. They had to shovel what was left of Drury into a sack.'

Kiegel seemed unconvinced. 'What about the Brits?'

Loovey turned his wrist, checking his watch. 'I'm seeing Arnold in thirty-five minutes. What do you want to do, stay here until I get back or what?'

Kiegel reached for his overcoat. 'You can give me a lift as far as a taxi. I'll take if from there and talk to you later.'

Loovey fastened the front door behind them. The lights were shining the length of the quiet residential street. Loovey opened the Cadillac. Kiegel sat beside him.

'When are you going back?' Loovey asked casually.

Kiegel replied with feeling. 'At eleven o'clock tomorrow morning. And I'd better take something with me that Fentiman will want to hear.'

Loovey dropped him off on the King's Road and continued to Brompton Square. Arnold answered the doorbell, dressed in the same mustard-coloured suit and sagging cardigan. A fire burned in the sitting room. *The Times* lay on the carpet, back page uppermost. The crossword puzzle had been completed. Arnold closed the door to the hall. His displeasure was plain.

'I thought we had an understanding,' he said severely. '"No flak", to use your own expression.'

Loovey was primed for the interview but he had a feeling that it was going to be even worse than he expected.

'It was a mistake,' he lied. 'Someone goofed. I'm sorry.'

Arnold pushed aside the apology. 'It's just not good enough! We're not used to this sort of behaviour. I mean blowing the car up, two separate police forces involved. Have you any idea at all of the trouble you're causing?'

'I'm sorry,' Loovey repeated. 'I accept full responsibility.'

The older man's cheeks coloured. 'Bugger you and your apologies!' he boomed. 'There'll be a lot of questions asked about this bloody nonsense and I'll have to provide the answers. Did Drury know where he was going?'

Loovey shifted his weight with caution, hiding his impatience.

'With respect, sir, he had to know where he was going. But he didn't know exactly where until the last half-hour. I picked him up at nine-thirty in the morning and I stayed with him all day. There's no possibility of him having been in touch with anyone else, if that's what you mean.'

'I'd better put you in the picture.' Arnold's deep voice spoke in measured strophes. 'That man you found in the manor grounds is an ex-detective inspector at Scotland Yard. He resigned a few years ago. He's been making a nuisance of himself ever since.'

A jet droned above, beginning its descent to Heathrow. Loovey said nothing.

Arnold seemed glad to continue. 'There's more to come. Raven and his wife were close friends of Drury and his girlfriend. And there's another mutual friend, a solicitor called Patrick O'Callaghan. He's Drury's executor. Are you getting the drift?'

The news was disturbing. Loovey nibbled on a cuticle.

'Is there any way the coroner's verdict could be upset?' he asked after a while.

Arnold's look was superior. 'No. When we do something we do it properly. That verdict's sealed like a tomb. What you have to ask yourself is what Raven was doing down at Capel Manor.'

'I have,' said Loovey.

Arnold shifted a coal with a pair of tongs. His face was shining when he straightened his back.

'Drury's blown to pieces one day. The following day Raven's found skulking round a house eleven miles away. Do you think that's coincidence?'

The implication multiplied with the speed of some deadly bacillus. Loovey made an instinctive gesture of rejection.

'I know the way Drury's mind worked. He wouldn't have told anyone what he was doing. In any case he didn't have the chance. There *has* to be another reason for Raven's involvement.'

Arnold showed old hound's teeth. 'When you discover it be

sure to let me know. In the meantime, my advice to you is to pack your bags and leave quickly.'

Loovey's guess was that Arnold was bluffing. The British were too deeply involved to ignore what could develop into a major scandal.

'You're making a big deal out of Drury,' he said. 'But you haven't asked a thing about Battaglia.'

'There's a good reason for that,' said Arnold. 'I'd rather not know.' He offered his canine grin again. 'I've been trying to make up my mind about you.'

'It's a common phenomenon,' Loovey said easily.

Arnold continued unmoved. 'Your strategy's tiptop. It's your tactics that worry me.'

'It's probably lack of experience,' Loovey said straightfaced.

'Probably,' Arnold agreed. He opened a drawer in the table and passed a large envelope to Loovey. 'This is a copy of Raven's personal file at the Yard. It'll give you some idea of the sort of man you're dealing with. It's all there, family background, schooling, service-record. There's a list of his known friends and associates. The trouble is that it tells you little about the man himself.'

Loovey glanced at the typewritten pages, put them back in the envelope, folded it twice and pushed it into his pocket.

'You wanted information about him,' said Arnold. 'You've got as much as I can get.'

'Tell me something,' said Loovey. 'Can his phone be bugged?'

'It could be,' said Arnold. 'But I strongly advise against it. He has a wide circle of friends, some of them in a position to cause even more trouble. How long are you thinking of staying in this country?'

'That depends,' answered Loovey. 'Why do you ask?'

Arnold touched another switch and the room came to light.

'Because the longer you stay the more likely it is that Raven will find you.'

Loovey allowed himself a short laugh. 'I think you're over-reacting, sir. You'll find I'm quite capable of taking care of people like Raven.'

'I doubt it,' said Arnold. 'The man is a walking time-bomb. You won't find that in the stuff I've just given you, but you can take it as gospel.'

Loovey brushed his trousers and came to his feet. 'You've made your point, sir, and I'm grateful for all you've done. I'll keep you informed, of course.'

Arnold accompanied him into the hall. 'You know the best thing you can do for me?'

It was said in a deep whisper and Loovey found himself responding. 'Anything at all, sir.'

'Call me from the United States,' said Arnold and closed the door.

Loovey drove straight to the Savoy. He was shown up to a room high above the river. Kiegel was in his shirtsleeves. Loovey lost no time in producing the envelope. Kiegel sat on the bed and read the contents.

He glanced up, shaking his head. 'What are you going to do about this guy?'

'For the moment, nothing,' he said. 'I need a little time to work something out. Arnold thinks that Raven knows Drury was at the manorhouse. He could be right.'

The nick on Kiegel's throat was bleeding again. He touched it with his finger and inspected the result.

'You think there's a chance that he got inside? Inside the house, I mean.'

The possibility worried Loovey continuously. 'I don't see how. The doors were locked back and front and he couldn't have seen into the hall.'

'What about the bloodstains on the floor?'

'I took a new rug down with me. Hansen's telling the servants that someone threw up on the old one.'

'What about the car that fetched Battaglia from the station?'

'No problem,' said Loovey. 'How many people knew that Joe was in England? You know anyone who's going to be looking for him?' He took back Raven's file.

'True,' allowed Kiegel. The lighting in the room imparted a greenish hue to his suntanned features. 'What's the bottom line on this joker, Phil? What's the worst he can do?'

'That's what I'm going to find out,' replied Loovey. 'And if it's bad he'll be stopped. I'm staying a few more days to take care of it.'

Kiegel looked at him, tapping a cigarette from the pack.

'Don't take this the wrong way, Phil, but it's no time for you to be fucking up.'

'You can only do your best.' Loovey regretted having said it as soon as he had spoken. It was an admission of weakness.

Kiegel jumped on it. 'There's no such thing as doing your best, not in this racket. Success is the only acceptable result.'

Loovey straightened his tie in the looking-glass. There was a bottle of duty-free Seagram on the bedside table. He poured himself a drink from it.

'Washington's been after Battaglia for six years. I delivered him. That's not what I call a fuck-up.'

'You're right,' said Kiegel. 'But I know what Fentiman's going to say. He's going to say that we can't afford to draw fire. And he's right, Phil.'

'I'll survive,' Loovey said shortly.

Kiegel used the bathroom and came out wiping his hands.

'I've confirmed my flight for tomorrow morning. What do I say to Fentiman?'

Loovey eyed him steadily. He had a shrewd idea that Kiegel would light a fire under his tail the moment he returned to Washington.

'Tell him everything's under control,' said Loovey.

Kiegel sat on the bed and kicked off his shoes, 'And Raven?'

Loovey's reply was deliberate. 'If Raven looks for trouble and comes too close, I'll make sure that he gets it. You can tell Fentiman that. Have a good flight, Ken.'

The chauffeur downstairs gave Loovey the keys to the Cadillac. He drove back to the house in Hurlingham. Lights upstairs told him that someone was at home. He stood at the foot of the stairs, listening to the blast of music coming from Shaky Jake's bedroom. He called but nobody answered. He walked up the stairs and glanced into Stepka's room. A bag lay open on the bed, partially packed. A passport and air ticket were on the dressing table. A photograph of an attractive woman was tucked into the frame of the looking-glass. Loovey went downstairs again. Kiegel was right, he thought, looking round. They lived like pigs. He read the newspaper that Kiegel had left behind until a taxi drew up outside. Stepka came into the room, rubbing his hands together. His face bore the expression of a man who was feeling the cold.

He stopped short, looking at Loovey. 'Something wrong?' he asked.

'Get that clown down here,' said Loovey. 'I want to talk to you both.'

Stepka bawled from the foot of the stairs. The racket stopped. The negro appeared, trailing a strong smell of hash. He was wearing a red and grey sweater, baggy trousers with elasticated bottoms and basketball boots. He swung a leg over a chair and sprawled on it. The two men waited for Loovey to speak.

'You're both booked out for tomorrow afternoon, right?' he said.

Shaky Jake was first to answer. 'Fifteen-twenty, American Airlines to Chicago.'

Loovey turned to Stepka. 'How about you?'

The fat man shifted uncomfortably. 'I'm on the waiting list.'

'Get yourself off it,' said Loovey. 'Something's come up.'

Shaky Jake smiled amiably. The pupils of his eyes were smaller than usual.

'Ain't nothing come up for me, man. I'm going home.'

'You can go where the hell you like,' answered Loovey. 'I'm talking to Stepka.'

Shaky Jake dropped a little lower on his shoulder blades, feeling for his nose with three fingers.

'There's something we've got to take care of,' Loovey said to Stepka.

The fat man moistened his lips with the end of his tongue.

'I've done what I'm getting paid for.'

The negro grinned. 'He's worried about his old lady.'

'Get out of here,' said Loovey. 'You're stoned.'

'A little bush,' said the negro. 'Nothing I can't handle.'

'I said get out of here,' said Loovey. 'And cut out the goddam soul music. We've got neighbours.'

The negro gathered his tattered dignity and unwound his long legs. 'I blew that turkey away,' he said. 'We ought to have a little respect around here.'

'Just go to bed,' said Loovey. 'We want you up early in the morning looking your button-bright best. And you can clean up this place before you leave. It's like a pig sty.'

'Respect,' Shaky Jake repeated. His eyes were like chestnuts swimming in glycerine. He danced to the foot of the stairs and his bedroom door slammed.

'OK,' said Loovey quietly. It was time for a change of pace. He opened the drinks cupboard. A light shone on the bottles inside.

'You want a drink?' he asked over his shoulder.

Stepka unbuttoned his jacket. His plump face was wary.

'Give me a vodka on the rocks.'

Ice rattled into the glass. Loovey carried it across the room. He helped himself to a weak rye-and-dry. Stepka poked at the ice cubes in his glass with thick fingers.

'If you're having problems at home, maybe we can work something out,' Loovey said quietly.

It was a while before Stepka answered. 'I'm forty-eight years old. Sonia's thirty.'

Loovey grinned. 'That's a dream come true, not a problem! Get on the phone,' he said pointing at the table against the wall. 'Call her! Tell her that you'll be home for sure at the end of the week. Tell her you're bringing her something special, that you're getting a bonus.'

Stepka put his glass down and wiped his hand across his wet lips. 'This is weird. I stay and the spade gets to go home.' The statement was larded with resentment.

'I'll make it up to you,' Loovey said quickly. 'I need your help; I need your brains. Take a look at this.' He passed Raven's file to the other man.

111

Stepka donned a pair of reading spectacles. He followed the text on the typewritten pages, his mouth forming the words soundlessly. When he finished, he raised his head.

'Who is this guy?'

'You just read it,' said Loovey. 'An ex-cop. I found him down at the house yesterday. I thought he was a reporter. I took the film in his camera and let him go. What you've just read has been given to me since.'

Stepka pursed his lips and let go with a long, low whistle.

'What the hell was he doing there?' He returned the envelope.

Loovey drew out the passport-size picture of Raven and gave it back to the fat man.

'I want you to get this guy's face fixed in your head,' he said.

Stepka studied the picture dubiously. 'What was he *doing* there?' he repeated.

Loovey's secret thought became words. 'I've got an idea Drury might have called him either before or after he went into that house.'

'You mean told him he was going to blow someone away?'

'No.' And this was still part of Loovey's thinking. 'For some other reason.'

The fat man gave the matter brief consideration; then his face cleared. 'If the guy doesn't know what went down I don't see the problem.'

Loovey leaned forward. 'I'll tell you the real problem. It's a sixty-five year old Englishman who didn't want us here in the first place, someone who doesn't like what we've done. He *knows* that Raven means trouble. This thing could escalate unless we're careful. That's why we've got to stop Raven.'

The fat man sat perfectly still, like a statue of Buddha. Finally his mouth opened.

'I'm not too sure that I understand.'

'I want you to check him out,' said Loovey. 'I want you to know who he sees, where he goes. You can rent a car, two cars – whatever you need. It's important that he doesn't know that he's being tailed. Here!'

The sketch he gave the fat man showed the river between Battersea and Albert Bridge, the flotilla of boats moored alongside Cheyne Walk. Loovey indicated the last boat.

'It's called the *Albatross*. He drives a grey Saab. XR 2984 W.'

Stepka's expression was dubious. 'I don't know,' he said doubtfully.

'You won't be working with the spade any more,' Loovey urged. 'So not a word to him, understand?'

Stepka put his spectacles in their case. 'I thought we had help here. Why don't they take care of it?'

'You're asking too many goddam questions,' said Loovey. 'Just do what I'm telling you, right? We don't ask for more help because we don't *need* more help. I'll call you at six o'clock tomorrow morning.'

It was the first time that the two men had ever shaken hands.

IO

Raven went out on deck dressed in his dressing-gown and pyjamas. It was still dark and bitterly cold. The river was stained by the reflections from the tall lamps along the Embankment. Traffic was sparse, little more than the occasional truck lumbering west on its way from the Channel ports. Raven collected the newspapers from the box at the end of the gangplank. The mail had not yet arrived. He made himself tea and went back to bed. The weather forecast on the radio spoke of a depression on its way from Iceland with the threat of more snow. Raven settled himself with the mug of tea. Oil-fired heating and double-glazing made the boat snug in a city that was fast in the grip of winter. He read both newspapers, looking for a reference to Drury's death or the coroner's inquest. There was nothing. The newspapers fell to the floor. He locked both hands behind his head and stared at the ceiling.

This need to keep news of Drury's death quiet proved that the authorities were in some way involved in it. He dug deeper in the same vein. The UK was high on the list of countries that were popular with terrorists. Maybe Drury had stumbled into something that he should never have known. The details of his death might provide a clue. But without reading a transcript of the evidence given at the inquest these would remain a mystery. And even then ... The circumstances bore the earmarks of an IRA outrage. First the explosion and the muzzled press, then the conspiracy of silence while the authorities planned their next move.

The letter he had found in the bedroom at Capel Manor forced its way into his mind. Surely the fact that Hansen was an arms dealer was more than coincidence. The more he thought about it, the more certain he was that Hansen was his lead. The pigskin travelling clock beside him showed twenty minutes to eight. He reached for the phone and composed Maggie Sanchez's number. Kirstie answered.

'Maggie's still sleeping,' she whispered. 'Don't hang up. I'll take it downstairs.' Seconds passed and she lifted the extension. 'She's feeling a whole lot better. I think she's coming to terms with things. Patrick called last night. Maggie wants George cremated. The service is next Monday, Putney Crematorium.'

The thought of his friend's remains being consumed in an electric furnace was not a pleasant one. People seemed in a hurry to destroy them along with his memory. He kept his thoughts to himself.

'How long are you going to stay over there?' he asked.

'A couple of days more at least. I'm trying to get Maggie to come away with us for a bit but she's being obstinate. She's been on the phone to her agent. She wants to work. It's crazy.'

'We'll talk her out of it,' he promised. It was ironic to think that George's death would finally get them into the sun.

Her voice came quickly. 'Hey, before I forget it. An American called for George last night. I talked to him.'

Raven's tone sharpened. 'What did he want?'

'Nothing in particular,' his wife replied. 'He said he was just passing through. He sounded shocked when I told him what had happened. He asked about Maggie.'

'Did she know who he was?'

'He didn't give a name. Just said how sorry he was and hung up. The phone never stopped ringing. I took it off the hook in the end. What are you up to?'

'This and that,' he said vaguely. 'I'm still in bed.'

She made a sound of mock disgust. 'Four million people are trying to get to work in this filthy weather and you're still in bed! Aren't you ashamed of yourself?'

'Not a bit,' he said cheerfully. 'Do you happen to know where that new shirt of mine is, the one you don't like?'

'It's in the airing cupboard in the bathroom,' she said, 'waiting for Mrs Burrows to sew on a button.' Kirstie neither sewed nor darned, not even for herself. 'Is that all you wanted?'

'That just about covers it,' he said. 'Except for the kiss on the end of your nose. Bye-bye.'

He went into the bathroom. The missing button had already been replaced, the shirt ironed. The pattern was grey and black stripes. He wore the shirt on principle, dressing in what Kirstie called his banking clothes. The grey herringbone tweed suit was twenty years old like most of the suits he'd had made for him. He wore it with a pair of black wingtip shoes. He was never quite in or out of fashion. He waited for the lights and then made a quick dash across the Embankment, which was busy now with the morning rush. The Saab motor fired with Swedish reliability. The anonymous call to Maggie's house intrigued him. He drove out of the cul-de-sac into the eastbound traffic. A voice on the radio warned that a lorry had shed its load at the north end of Chelsea Bridge. There was a tail-back. He turned left at Royal Hospital Road and filtered through Chelsea and Victoria into a maze of one-way streets and hidden turnings that lay between St James's Palace and Piccadilly. He left the Saab in a parking place reserved for palace personnel, a DISABLED card on the ledge under the windscreen. The address on the letter he had seen in the country was lodged in his head. The house was Georgian and bore a plaque on the outside wall: ADMIRAL JOHN CRAVEN LIVED HERE 1806-1822.

The hall was a mixture of old and new. A mural in the manner of Fragonard and bronze-faced Siemens lifts. A man wearing the uniform of the Corps of Commissionaires was sitting in a sedan chair facing the entrance. He looked up as Raven approached.

'Good morning, sir, can I help you?'

'I'm looking for the offices of Sven Hansen,' said Raven.

The man pointed across the hall. Raven turned the brass door-handle.

The room was long, with an oil-painting of a man in a plumed hat hanging above an Adam fireplace. A woman was sitting behind a period walnut desk. There was a striped sofa on her left and a low table littered with magazines. Correspondence in front of her failed to conceal the copy of the *Tatler* she was reading.

'Good morning,' she said in a Betty Boop voice. She was in her late thirties and wearing a grey suit. Her blonde hair was cut in peaks over her ears.

'Mr Hansen?' Raven asked, smiling.

She studied him with interest. 'I'm afraid Mr Hansen isn't here.'

'Really?' Raven turned towards a closed door on the other side of the room. 'I'm supposed to have an appointment with him.'

Her expression was as puzzled as his. 'I'm sorry, I didn't catch your name.'

'Of course,' he said quickly. 'John Raven.'

She shook her head, long earrings swinging. She opened a leather-bound diary and ran a finger down the entries.

'I don't seem to see your name down here, Mr Raven. I don't understand.'

He made a show of embarrassed confusion. 'I'd be the first to admit that my memory isn't all that it should be, but it can't be as bad as that. John Raven from Toronto. As a matter of fact I called Mr Hansen at his home in the country only yesterday but there was no answer.'

That too puzzled her. 'There should have been somebody there. What time would this be, Mr Raven?'

'Six, seven o'clock. I can't remember exactly.'

'And when do you say you made your appointment? It couldn't have been through me or I'd have a record of it.'

'No, this was done with Mr Hansen himself a couple of weeks ago. I've come over specially.'

'This is weird,' she said. 'I'm surprised that Mr Hansen didn't say anything to me before he left at least. He's usually very good about appointments. Almost Germanic.' The description seemed to please her. 'Let me get you some tea,' she said quickly. 'Milk and sugar?'

'Milk and sugar would be fine.'

Wariness flooded into his brain as she loped across the room, her skirt clinging to her figure. For a moment he thought that

117

the offer of tea was no more than a ruse to get past him, that she was about to open a door to the hall and scream for help. She opened a cupboard and took out an electric kettle, cups and a packet of digestive biscuits. Her manner turned his visit into a social occasion. She made the tea, pouring with the utmost refinement. She retreated behind her desk and looked at him, clicking her tongue.

'I wish I knew what to suggest,' she said. 'What a nuisance.'

His forehead creased in a frown. 'To say the least. If he's not here or in the country, where the hell is he?'

His abruptness startled her into indiscretion. 'Mr Hansen's in Belgium. I'm afraid he'll be there for another ten days.'

He shook his head despondently and then, as though struck by a sudden thought, asked, 'Do you have a number for him there?'

Her eyes were uncertain. 'I do, but he left strict instructions. I'm not supposed to call him except in a case of emergency.'

'This *is* an emergency,' he insisted.

'But it's not what he meant. I know it isn't. Mr Hansen's in Belgium on private business and he doesn't want to be disturbed.'

'This is ridiculous,' Raven said. 'I've come three thousand miles and I can't even speak to him?'

His indignation seemed to impress her. 'If you could give me some idea,' she faltered. 'I mean, the nature of your business, maybe I could help you myself.'

'You ought to know better than that,' he said tartly.

It took courage to make her decision. 'If you'll take the responsibility you can call him yourself.'

She pushed the telephone across the desk. He dialled, substituting a six for the five on the paper. A meaningless buzz in his ear resulted.

He repeated the charade and put the phone down. 'There's no answer. I'll try later from my hotel. And don't worry, I'll tell Mr Hansen how helpful you've been.'

She scribbled the number on a pad, tore off the sheet and gave it to him.

'I hope we meet again,' he said courteously.

'I hope so too,' she replied. Her eyes followed him to the door.

He used a pay-phone near the railings of Green Park. The booth was out of sight of the building he had just left. A man's voice said, 'Yes?'

'Mr Hansen?'

'Who is this?' The accent was mid-Atlantic.

'George Drury, I'm trying to get hold of him. I was told you could help me.'

The connection was broken abruptly as if a hand-grenade the man was holding had just had the pin pulled.

Raven walked back to the car. He had just been given his answer or part of it. No matter how tenuous the link between Hansen and Drury was, it existed. A wind had got up. By the time Raven reached the Embankment, falling snow obscured the south bank of the river.

He found the *Directory of Directors* again. A second look gave him little more information other than that the company had been founded in 1969. He returned the book to its shelf. All he knew about arms dealing was that fortunes were made from second-hand weapons. Out of date armaments were sold to Third World countries, some of them rich from oil revenues.

There was a strong smell of furniture polish on the boat. Mrs Burrows had been and gone. He found the usual note in the kitchen. There was steak-and-kidney pudding in the freezer. He dropped it over the side for the fish that were returning to the Thames. It was difficult to tell her that he no longer needed her cooking. She viewed his marriage as a deliberate act of self-destruction.

There was only one call on the Ansafone. It was from Jerry Soo. 'Meet me at half-past five in Tristan's. It's important.'

Raven left the boat at five, sheltered under a golf umbrella. The wine-bar was only four hundred yards away on Chelsea Green. A failed actor ran it, an extrovert who treated his customers as a captive audience. Raven placed his umbrella in the stand and took a seat with a glass of house champagne. It was too early for the proprietor and his cronies, the Hooray Henrys and Knightsbridge secretaries. The place was empty

119

except for the barman and Jerry Soo.

The Chinese cop shifted his can of Coke. 'Annie Barr, remember her?'

Raven tried and turned his mouth down. 'No.'

Soo's range of facial expressions was limited to a broad grin and a look of complete inscrutability. 'A tall, dark girl,' he said, 'not bad looking. We met her at the airport a couple of years ago. When we were going fishing in Norway.'

The memory built up. 'Got it,' said Raven. 'She worked at the Yard. Something to do with traffic-control.'

'She moved,' said Soo. 'She's working in CI Eleven. Somebody in Personnel asked for your file yesterday. I met her in the canteen and she told me. She remembered you.'

The blood ran a little faster in Raven's veins. 'My file's been pulled out before.'

'Not by the Commissioner's Office. Not for some time, at least.' Soo's body gave the impression that it was made of hard rubber covered with fabric. 'I make it my business to keep an ear to the ground where you're concerned. I like to know of the trouble I could be landing myself in. Your file was collected by a messenger from the Home Office.'

Raven leaned forward propped on both elbows. His voice was quiet. 'And what do you think that means?' He had a shrewd idea but he needed it confirmed.

Soo rolled on his seat. 'The rules haven't changed. Personal files aren't supposed to leave the premises under any circumstances. They made a copy and they took a picture. You know where that file went?'

Raven lowered his voice. There was no one else there but the barman. 'Some sort of security agency?'

'You're damn right!' said his friend. 'Some sort of security agency. It's George Drury, isn't it?'

Raven held the other man's look for a moment, then nodded. 'It has to be.'

The Chinaman breathed hard through his nose. 'We've known one another for seventeen years. Have I ever given you any foolish advice?'

'No,' Raven admitted.

'Then listen to me now, John. Walk away from this business while you can. Don't mess with it. Walk away before they decide to teach you a lesson for once and for all.'

'*They*,' Raven repeated.

'That's right,' said his friend. 'The people who make the rules. The ones who sit in high places. Pay attention to what I'm telling you for once. Believe me, I know.'

There was no doubt of the other man's concern and sincerity, but Raven was unconvinced.

'Drury wasn't a friend of yours.'

Soo's boot-button eyes were unwinking. 'No, but you are.'

'If I told you the truth you probably wouldn't believe me,' said Raven.

'I might,' said Soo. 'In fact I probably would. But my advice would still be the same.'

Raven drank the remains of the drink in his glass. 'Let's not talk about it any more, Jerry. I'm going to do what I think I should do and that's all there is to it. You're better off out of it. You're in the firing line as it is.'

Soo seemed reluctant to let him go. 'Is Kirstie involved in all this?'

Raven shook his head. 'The only other person who knows is Patrick O'Callaghan. I'm trying to keep it like that. George is being cremated on Monday.'

'Where's Kirstie now?' asked Soo.

'She's staying with Maggie Sanchez for a couple of days.'

'OK,' said Soo, coming to his feet. 'If you want me I'll be at home. Just take care of yourself.'

Raven walked back to the river under his umbrella. He unlocked his car. Soo's news had disturbed him, but his resolve was unweakened. He had to return to the house in the country and find out whatever he could. He switched on the motor. The fuel-gauge showed no more than a quarter full. He drove round the block to his usual filling-station. The attendant busied himself with Raven's windscreen, snapping his cleaning-leather. Raven felt for a tip. He drove out with an eye on the rear-view mirror. A Toyota with its lights on was parked twenty yards away. It was still behind him as he drove into the anarchy of the roundabout system beyond Wandsworth Bridge. Whoever was driving the Toyota was good at his job, keeping four and five vehicles between his own car and the one he was tailing. The grim outline of the prison loomed on his right. The road narrowed now, reduced to two lanes as it crossed Wandsworth Common. Raven braked suddenly, pulling in to the kerb. He stood by the side of the Saab, affecting an interest in the near back wheel. The Toyota passed without slackening speed. It turned left after a hundred yards. Raven guessed that the driver had parked out of sight and was waiting to continue the chase. He swung the Saab into an illegal U-turn and trod on the accelerator, travelling fast down the hill past the cemetery. The next glance up at the mirror showed a clear road behind him.

The snow had stopped by the time he reached open country. He swung left and the headlights shone through the trees lining the lane. The white-painted gate was latched open. Raven drove through on to the drive. The front of the house was in darkness. He left the Saab on the gravelled turning-circle and walked into the stableyard. The garage was open. A small estate car stood beside the Corniche. Lights showed behind the kitchen curtains. Raven rapped on the door with his knuckles. The door opened as far as a length of chain would allow. A woman peered out, clutching the top of her housecoat. She called, seeing Raven, and a man took her place. He was in his fifties, with suspicious eyes and wearing a roll-neck sweater and baggy flannel trousers. The woman was close behind him.

'What do you want?' the man asked brusquely.

'Is Mr Hansen in?' Raven said politely.

The man looked past Raven into the yard, making sure that there was no one else there.

'He's not here,' he snapped.

'When do you expect him back?' Raven persisted.

The woman whispered something in the man's ear. 'Who are you?' he demanded. 'What's your business here?'

'I'm trying to get in touch with Mr Hansen,' said Raven.

'Bugger off or I'll call the police.' The door was slammed and the bolts were rammed home.

II

Loovey closed the door behind him. The house in Hurlingham was empty. Stepka had not yet returned. It was five minutes to ten. A red light at the base of the wall in the sitting room glowed. He unlocked the safe and lifted out the computerised scramble-phone. The sophisticated system changed the code automatically every five seconds. A button allowed the user to shift from scramble to clear. Loovey took the phone to the sofa. It was Fentiman on the line. His voice was dangerously quiet.

'Just what the hell's going on over there? I've got Kiegel God knows where and all sorts of shit flying at me from the Brits. What's happening, Loovey?'

Loovey cleared his throat. 'Kiegel's in his hotel, sir. He's flying back tomorrow with a full report.'

'I don't give a rat's ass about Kiegel's report,' said Fentiman. 'This is serious stuff, Loovey. You're in charge and I want you to tell me. What's happening about this Raven?'

Loovey was grateful that three thousand miles separated them.

'He managed to get hold of Hansen's secretary. She gave him Hansen's number in Belgium.'

'You're damn right she did,' screamed Fentiman. 'Hansen's shouting his head off and I don't wonder at it. He's not going to want it known that he's the guy who set up Battaglia. It's not exactly healthy in his line of business. What happened, Loovey?'

Loovey fixed his eyes on a point in the ceiling. Fentiman was nowhere near finished.

'Raven asked Hansen about Drury. That means he knows that there's a connection. It doesn't matter that he's got it wrong. This bastard's getting closer all the time. What did Arnold tell you?'

'Not a lot, sir. He gave me Raven's file.'

'When was that?'

'Yesterday. That's the last time I was in touch with him.'

'Damn right!' bawled Fentiman. 'He doesn't know how to get hold of you. You haven't been in your hotel. Where *have* you been, Loovey?'

'Making some enquiries, sir.'

'Shit,' said Fentiman. 'The thing is, Arnold knows how to get hold of me. He's firing all this stuff through the air about Drury *et cetera*. He claims you've kicked over a hornets' nest there. They've had to invoke special measures to keep the wraps on this business. And it still isn't over. Raven has to be stopped, Loovey.'

'I've got it in hand, sir.'

'Is that so,' Fentiman said sarcastically. 'Well let me tell you something that isn't in hand. There's been a reporter from the *Post* down in Virginia asking questions of Battaglia's sister.'

A sudden feeling of nausea flooded Loovey's stomach. 'It has to be a coincidence, sir,' he said quickly. 'Joe's been news for years. I can assure you that there's been no leak over here. There's not even an official record of Battaglia having been in the country. He came on a false book. As far as the British are concerned he never existed.'

Fentiman's voice vaulted the Atlantic and snarled in Loovey's face. 'I want this Raven stopped, Phil. I want him stopped fast. Do you understand?'

'I'll want clearance,' said Loovey.

'Did you say "clearance"?' Fentiman demanded.

'That's right, sir.' Loovey's tone was dogged. 'For what I had in mind.'

Fentiman rose to a pinnacle of icy politeness. 'You're the case officer, Phil. You're in charge. I want to hear no more nonsense about clearance. Have you still got those people of yours over there?'

'One of them, sir. I sent the other one back.'

Fentiman changed yet again. 'Listen to me, Phil. I'm relying on you and this is no bullshit. Do you need Kiegel to stay on?'

'Kiegel's the last person I need,' Loovey said with feeling. 'I want him off my back.'

'OK, then. Use whatever you've got but I want a result. I want a result within the next twenty-four hours. Is that firmly fixed in your head, Phil?'

'It is,' answered Loovey. He put the scramble-phone back in the wall-safe, locked it away and went back to the sofa.

A car drew up outside shortly after eleven. Stepka slouched in to the sitting room carrying his weight as if exhausted. He made straight for the drinks cupboard, half-filled a glass with vodka, added ice and thudded down on the sofa.

'I lost the bastard.'

Loovey said nothing.

Stepka was sweating heavily in spite of the cold outside. He unfastened his tie and collar.

'The guy's street-smart. He knows all the angles.'

'He was a cop,' said Loovey, 'or did you forget?'

'He stopped so I stopped,' the man said heavily. 'By the time I turned round he was long gone. No sign of him.'

There was nobody else in the house but the two of them, but Loovey closed the door to the hall.

'I want you to tell me something,' he said. 'Think hard before you answer. A lot depends upon it. Do you think he made you? Do you think he'd recognise you if he saw you again?'

Stepka leaned both hands on his knees as though filling himself with assurance. 'No. No, that much I'm certain of.' His eyes were steady as they met Loovey's inspection.

'When was this?' asked Loovey. 'When did you lose him?'

'About half-past six. I drove back to the pub opposite the boat. You can see the river from the windows. I called you here but there was no reply. He came back half-an-hour ago, so I left.'

There's a change of plan,' said Loovey. 'We're going to take the guy out.'

Stepka closed his eyes. 'Oh, boy!' he said softly.

'There's a five thousand dollar bonus in it for you,' said Loovey. 'Did you call your wife last night?'

The fat man wagged his head despondently.

'Where's she staying?' asked Loovey.

'Stonington, Connecticut. A hotel called the Harbour.'

'Have you got the number?'

The fat man produced a slip of paper. 'Yes.'

Loovey picked up the phone from the table and dialled the number. Once it was ringing he handed the instrument to Stepka.

'Tell her you'll be home the day after tomorrow. For sure.'

He left the room as the fat man started to speak. He used the bathroom upstairs. An attempt had been made to clean the place. The blankets and sheets on the negro's bed had been neatly folded, the ashtrays emptied. He flushed the cistern and went down the stairs again. The fat man was off the phone.

'OK?' said Loovey.

'Yes,' said Stepka. 'She was on her way out. I said what you told me. She sounded pleased.'

'She would be,' smiled Loovey. He had found the fat man six months after Stepka had been released from Leavenworth. Stepka's parole obligations had finished the moment that Loovey took over. The fat man's sheet had come with him. There was little about the ex-con that Loovey didn't know. A second-time loser, he had shot and wounded a Federal Bank employee. He had served eight years, making parole on his second appearance. He had worked on and off for Loovey ever since. His wife was comparatively new, a cocktail waitress he had met in a Baltimore bar.

Loovey re-opened the safe. He pulled out the plastic shopping bag, pulled a table between his chair and Stepka's and put the bag on the table between them. The two men looked at one another then Loovey opened the shopping bag. The small hand-made pistol had a trigger-button. A compressed-air cartridge in the butt provided the fire-power.

'This thing's got a muzzle velocity of three hundred feet a second,' said Loovey. 'That's clout!'

He shook out a tiny platinum-headed pellet from a phial. It was notched at one end and had the dimension of a knitting needle. He used his handkerchief to protect his fingers as he loaded the pellet into the firing chamber. A safety-catch prevented mishap. He extended the weapon in the palm of his hand.

'All you need is one shot but you've got to be close to him. Less than a yard. Hit him anywhere. The back's as good a place as any.'

Stepka continued to stare, making no move to take the weapon from Loovey. 'I don't know,' he muttered.

Loovey put the loaded weapon back in the wall-safe. He came back across the room, smiling.

'How do you mean you don't know, Ben?'

The fat man shifted uneasily. 'I'm taking a big chance here.'

'Garbage,' said Loovey. 'You're in and you're out. By the time the body's found you'll be back in New York.'

'I don't know,' Stepka repeated. 'I thought we had help here.'

'We've got help we don't use,' answered Loovey. 'And do you know why we don't use it, Ben? Because this is something between you and me.'

'This isn't the goddam movies,' said Stepka.

Loovey leaned forward, finger upraised. 'We've been working together for some time now, Ben. Have I ever steered you wrong?'

The fat man looked uncomfortable. 'That's different. I've always known what I was doing.'

Loovey took him back in time. 'You never objected before,' he said gently. 'Two of them, Ben, remember. Don't tell me your conscience is bothering you.'

Stepka puffed out his cheeks. 'It isn't my goddam conscience. It's running around popping off at people with toy pistols.'

'This is no toy pistol,' answered Loovey. 'It's a highly sophisticated weapon. And a lethal one.'

Stepka's expression remained obstinate.

'What you're doing isn't just for yourself,' said Loovey. 'Have you stopped to think about that?'

Stepka blinked suspiciously. 'No, I can't say that I have. What are you talking about, anyway?'

'I'm talking about your wife,' said Loovey. 'You're doing it so that you can give her the things she wants, Ben. What's the alternative? Raven's put us all in the firing line. You, me, the people who give me my orders. And once you're in, you're in for good.'

Stepka's eyes slid away. 'When's all this supposed to take place?'

Loovey knew his man. Stepka was wavering. Loovey looked at his watch. It was just before eleven o'clock.

'In about seven hours' time,' he said. 'On the boat.'

Stepka was vehement. 'There isn't a chance that I'd get aboard that boat without being seen! Have you been there?'

'I've been there,' said Loovey. 'You don't go *on* the boat; you hit him outside. You say you're sure he won't recognise you?'

'He won't recognise me but he might know the car.'

'You won't be in the car,' said Loovey. 'You've got nothing to worry about, Ben, except me.'

'I don't understand,' said Stepka. 'Why do I have to worry about you?'

'One simple phone-call,' said Loovey, 'and you're back in the slammer. Parole revoked and a few more years on top. I'm sure that can be arranged.'

The fat man's face flushed. He looked stunned. 'Jesus Christ!' he said. 'So *this* is what it's all about!'

Loovey stretched across and grabbed Stepka's lapel, tugging it gently. 'What it's all about is a choice, Ben, and the choice is yours.'

He relinquished his grip. Stepka straightened his jacket. He spoke like a beaten man.

'What do you want me to do?'

'Get a good night's sleep, that's what I want you to do! I'm spending the night here.'

Something still concerned the fat man. He voiced his concern. 'Weather like this, how you going to get this joker out at six in the morning?'

'Don't be worried about that,' said Loovey. He opened the door to the hallway. 'Let's hit the sack,'

Stepka climbed the stairs very slowly. Loovey stayed in the

sitting room, listening to the sound of the fat man preparing for bed. Loovey was suddenly free from the pressure that had been building up around him. He was certain that the decision he had taken was the right one. He explored its ramifications. If things went right for him, the wrong conclusions would be drawn about Raven's death. On the other hand if luck didn't come his way, any suspicions engendered could never be proven. One way or another, Raven's removal would close the file on Battaglia.

He turned out the last light, went upstairs and put clean sheets on his bed. He undressed and lay in the darkness, listening to Stepka snoring. After a while, Loovey dozed. He had trained himself in the art of catnapping. It was five o'clock in the morning when he opened his eyes. He pulled on his trousers and banged on Stepka's door.

'Time to get up!' he called. 'I'm going to make some coffee.'

He shaved and finished dressing. The coffee and toast were made by the time Stepka came downstairs. They carried it into the sitting room. The curtains were partly open, showing a dark, ragged sky over the river. Loovey unlocked the wall-safe. He gave the gun to the fat man, still wrapped in the plastic shopping bag.

'Got your gloves?'

Stepka nodded across at his jacket. He was badly shaven and nervous. He dropped the shopping bag in his overcoat pocket.

'Wear your gloves,' said Loovey. 'And remember what I told you! Wait in the alleyway. There are no lights. He'll come from the boat. Don't waste any time. Just hit him and get the hell out of there. OK?'

The fat man struggled into his overcoat. 'You're sure he'll leave the boat?'

'He'll leave,' Loovey was confident. He opened the front door. The rented Toyota carried a powdering of snow. There were no lights in any of the neighbouring houses. Loovey lowered his voice.

'Don't forget. Sink the gun in the river and bury this car somewhere. Call me as soon as you've done your job.'

12

The noise was insistent, claiming Raven back from the shadowy world of dreams. He opened his eyes and reached for the phone. Sleep had deafened him to the creaking of timber, the monotonous thud as the hull of the boat bumped against the fenders. The voice on the phone spoke with an American accent.

'John Raven?'

Raven switched on the bedside lamp. It was a quarter to six by the travelling clock.

'Have you any idea of the time?' he demanded.

'Never mind the time,' said the voice. 'You're a friend of George Drury's, right?'

Raven straightened his back. 'Who is this speaking?'

'Let's not bother with names. You want to know the truth about Drury's death, correct?' There was a ring of confidence in the man's voice.

'Yes,' Raven said with caution.

'Then let's not waste one another's time. I'm sticking my neck out here. I can give you the facts about George's so-called accident and the proof to go with them.'

'Can I ask you a question?' said Raven.

'You get one free,' said the voice. 'The rest cost money.'

The boat rocked as Raven considered his next move. He chose the words carefully.

'George was murdered, wasn't he?'

'That doesn't come from the freebie bag. That's an expensive one.'

'How expensive?' asked Raven.

'It's negotiable. But we have to act fast. Can you meet me right away?'

Raven glanced sideways at the clock. 'Where?'

'You were on St James's Street yesterday, asking about someone who's in Belgium. Be there in half-an-hour's time. The front door will be open. Walk straight in.'

Raven hesitated. He was clearly talking to somebody close to Hansen. 'You mentioned money. There's no way I can get my hands on any at this hour in the morning.'

His caller was losing patience. 'Quit stalling, Raven. If you want the information we'll get the money. And come alone!'

Raven kicked off the duvet and ran into the bathroom. He pulled a razor over his face and pair of jeans over his long-johns. A heavy sweater and his lumberjacket completed his protection against the cold. There was no time to call anyone, little to say if he did. He opened a drawer in his desk, took out the Browning twenty-two and fastened it to his leg under his sock with a strip of adhesive tape. Snow drifted into his face, wet and cool as he walked along the deck. The rest of the boats lay in darkness. Nothing stirred. The tall lamp-standards overhead diffused light along the Embankment. The cul-de-sac where he parked the Saab was pitch black in comparison. There was no traffic at all. He ran across the road into the mouth of the dead-end. His car was facing the exit, the walls and the space around it in deep shadow. He was feeling in his pocket for his keys when a shape appeared from the back of the car. Raven dropped instinctively as the man raised his arm. There was a hiss like a valve releasing a jet of steam. Something pinged against the side of the car. Raven rolled on the ground, pulling the Browning out of his sock. He came up on his knees, ramming the barrel of the Browning against his assailant's stomach, forcing him back to the wall. Raven rose, keeping the gun where it was, his free hand reaching behind with the ignition-key. He managed to open the door. The interior lights came on revealing the fat man pinned against the wall. His hat and the weapon he had used were lying on the ground. Raven retrieved the tiny air-gun.

He stepped back cautiously, looking down as he felt something hard through the sole of his sneaker. He shifted his foot and bent again, retrieving the flattened scrap of metal. He put it in his pocket with the air-pistol. The man against the wall watched Raven's every move through deepset eyes sunk in a fleshy face. Raven closed the car door with a foot. It locked with a well-engineered click. He lifted the Browning.

'We're going to cross the street together. There's a flight of steps leading down to a door. Beyond the door there's a boat. That's where we're going. One wrong move and I'll put a bullet in you. I've had enough of you bastards!'

Headlights briefly swept the mouth of the cul-de-sac. Raven crowded his assailant deep into shadow until the lorry had lumbered past. There was no one to watch as the two men hurried across the road. The fat man went first down the steps, steadying his progress by clinging to the massive granite blocks. He stopped at the bottom, shoulders hunched as though expecting a blow from behind, his grizzled crewcut held low. Raven reached past him and unlocked the door to the gangplank. Both men made their way along the deck. Raven pulled the curtains and switched on the lights. The fat man was breathing heavily.

'Take your clothes off,' Raven ordered. 'Come on, all of them.'

The man glanced round the room, his eyes furtive. He made no move to obey.

Raven lifted the Browning again. 'I don't have a lot of patience,' he warned.

The fat man started to undress, dropping his clothes in front of him. He stopped at his pants and vest.

Raven waved the barrel of his gun. 'Everything!'

Naked, the man was grotesque. Rolls of fat covered his hips and shoulders. Limbs and body were completely devoid of hair. Raven opened the drawer in his desk. It contained souvenirs of his police service. A framed copy of his letter of resignation that had once hung in the lavatory, a sheaf of commendations, the roll of burglar tools and a pair of bulldog snappers, police-issue handcuffs.

'Put your hands behind your back,' he said to the man.

The fat man stood as Raven tightened the ratchet on the manacles. Raven pushed him down on a chair where he sat with his belly bulging over his genitals. His face was sullen and apprehensive.

'What's your name?' asked Raven. 'You're going to open that ugly mouth of yours,' Raven added when the man made no reply.

Raven picked up the man's overcoat. There was nothing in the pockets except a Hertz receipt for money paid in respect of a rented Toyota. The accompanying insurance cover was issued in the name of Salvatore Fiore with an address in south-west London. It was dated the previous day. Raven went through the suit jacket. The United States passport had been issued in the same name, Salvatore Fiore, born Albany New York, February 20, 1940. The title page carried the photograph of the man slumped in the chair. There was a wallet with a hundred odd pounds and 360 dollars. There were coins, a set of ignition-keys and some house keys, a packet of Camels and matches. Raven knocked the fat man's shoes on the floor, looking for anything that might have been hidden there.

'Is that your real name?' he asked.

The fat man spoke for the first time. The grossness of his naked body, the handcuffs, made a show of defiance difficult but he managed it somehow.

'You got any sense, friend, you'll take these cuffs off and start running. You're out of your league.'

Raven cocked his head. This was not the voice he had heard earlier on the phone. He switched on his powerful desk-lamp and studied the air-pistol and pellet under its light. The pistol was made of steel and plastic. A compressed-air cartridge provided the one-shot fire-power. The calibre of the weapon was the smallest Raven had ever come across. He placed the flattened pellet under his magnifying glass. The cavity in its head had collapsed. Two tiny holes were elongated. Raven straightened up, looking at the American through half-closed eyes. An almost forgotten memory clamoured for recognition. He stared down at his fingers in sudden alarm and ran for the bathroom. He held his hand under a stream of scalding water until he could bear it no longer. He dried his hands and inspected the skin closely for abrasions or punctures. There was no sign of either and his panic subsided. He went back to the sitting room. Outrage blurred his thinking. He stepped close and rocked the American's head with a backhanded blow.

'You bastard!' he said savagely. 'You're going to talk, I promise you!'

Blood trickled from the American's lip. The blow had reddened one side of his face. He explored his cut lip with the tip of his tongue.

'I talk to you, I'm a dead man,' he said.

The wind had freshened, rocking the boat. 'If you don't talk,' said Raven, 'you'll be inside for the rest of your life. Bank on it!'

The American bent awkwardly, wiping his cut mouth on his shoulder. 'I already told you. You're out of your league.'

Raven sensed the panic behind the bravado. He built on it.

'Is that your real name on that passport?'

The man moved his shoulders but not his mouth.

'OK, then, it isn't,' said Raven. 'So what do I call you, "fat man"?'

This time the man answered. 'Ben.'

'Ben?' Raven looked at him. 'OK, then, Ben. You've got your priorities wrong. Your friends aren't here. I am. You'll talk to me or you'll talk to the police. You've got thirty seconds to make your mind up which it is.'

He picked up the phone and consulted his watch. The American mumbled something then started again.

'You don't understand, do you?'

Rage rushed into Raven's voice. 'I understand all right. You killed George Drury and you tried to kill me. It doesn't take a lot of imagination to work that one out.'

'I had nothing to do with Drury.' The fat man's voice quivered with emotion. 'I never clapped eyes on the guy and that's the truth.'

'But you know who I'm talking about? Your time's up anyway.'

134

He dialled the first part of the police emergency number. The fat man spoke hurriedly.

'What's the matter, I'm talking, aren't I? Sure, I know who you mean but I didn't kill him. That was somebody else.'

It was a relief to know the truth at last, to be reassured that his hunch was right.

'Tell me about it,' said Raven, putting the phone down.

'Let me have a cigarette.' The man nodded at the pack on the desk.

Raven lit a Camel and stuck it in the fat man's mouth. The cigarette bobbed as the man spoke.

'What kind of deal are you offering?'

Raven laughed outright. 'Are you out of your mind, Ben? Sitting there cuffed with your belly hanging out and talking about deals!'

Ben flinched as hot ash fell on his bare chest. 'I've got to have something going for me. A chance to run. I'm dead the way it is.'

Raven removed the cigarette brusquely, leaving a shred of paper sticking to the other man's lip. The American spat it out.

'You're too cute to get breaks,' said Raven. 'A friend of mine has been murdered. A good man. I want whoever's responsible.'

'If they don't get you first.'

Raven lit a cigarette of his own. 'Let me take care of that. I've been listening hard and I haven't heard anything but wind. Who was that on the phone this morning, the guy who got me off the boat with that bullshit story? Is he the guy who's running you?'

The fat man answered a previous question. 'The guy who killed your friend is back in the States. He wired the car Drury was driving. And that's all I know about it, so help me God!'

Life was stirring in the other boats. Someone was practising scales on a clarinet. A baby was crying. There was a smell of breakfast cooking.

'Let's start again,' suggested Raven. 'Why was George Drury killed?'

135

The fat man's tongue touched his split lip. 'The guy I work for . . . Look, I do what I'm told and I don't ask questions. It's kept me alive.'

'Why was Drury killed?' Raven repeated.

The American's voice was almost inaudible. 'He knew too much.'

'Knew too much about what?'

'The way I heard it, he wasted someone for them. So they got rid of him. It's their style.'

The statement shocked Raven profoundly. 'Are you saying George Drury killed somebody?'

'Look, I've got to have something,' the man said urgently. 'I missed you, I cut my own throat. I've got a wife, Raven.'

'So have I,' Raven answered. 'Almost a widow. Who was this person Drury killed?'

'Someone who'd worked with them. They needed him dead. Your friend did the job for him.'

There was no doubt in Raven's mind that the fat man was telling the truth. Things began to take shape. Drury's trip to the States. The telephone calls. His sudden acquisition of money.

'Who gives you your orders?' he asked.

'You want a name, he's got twenty,' said the fat man. 'Like I told you, this is a different game, Raven. You're dealing with professionals.'

'You mean spooks. Who is it, CIA?'

The American shrugged. Raven bore down on him. 'Are you willing to repeat what you've just said to me?'

The American's grin was one-sided. 'What do you think this is, the Truth Game? I wouldn't make it to the stand.'

'I don't mean in court,' said Raven. 'I want the guy who ordered Drury's murder. The man who sent you here. Give him to me and you've got your chance to run.'

The fat man lifted his head. 'There's not a thing they don't know about you. Your wife, your friends, everything.'

'We all go through difficult times,' said Raven. He was close and he was getting closer. He had to keep pushing.

'Do you know what was in the pellet you fired at me?'

The fat man moved his head from side to side. 'Just to hit you from near. That's all he said. You're going to do something for me, right?'

Raven stared at him, cold-eyed. 'I'll tell you what I'd like to do for you. I'd like to put you over the side with your head up your arse. This is a simple equation, Ben. What I do for you depends on what you do for me.'

The phone shrilled, cutting into their conversation. It was Kirstie. 'I'm sorry, darling, did I wake you?'

'No,' he replied. 'I've been up for some time.'

'There's something wrong,' she challenged. 'Your voice sounds strange.'

'I've got someone here,' he said. The fat man was sweating.

'At this hour in the morning?' Then she laughed. 'Who is she?'

'It's someone who's here on business.'

Her tone cooled noticeably. 'Then if you can't talk to me can you talk to Maggie? She wants a word with you.'

'Can't you tell me what she wants?' he urged. 'I'm in the middle of something important, Kirstie.'

He heard his wife sigh. 'It's about the cremation. Maggie would like us to go together. Patrick, you, me and her. Emma Tufnell and people are making their own way there.'

Cremation was only three days away. Incinerating Drury's body would destroy the last physical evidence of the cause of his death. It was suddenly important that it should be stopped or at least postponed. Patrick would know the correct procedure. For the moment at least he was the only one who could be trusted.

'We'll talk about it later,' he promised. 'What are your plans now?'

'We're going out,' said his wife. 'Maggie has shopping to do and I have to look in at the studio. We'll be home for supper.'

'OK,' he answered. 'I'll call you then. Have there been any more phone-calls?'

'Just one from the insurance broker. He wanted a bill from Kutchinsky for Maggie's diamond earrings. You sound very odd to me, John. What's going on over there?'

He hid his nervousness with a show of irritation. 'I'll tell you what's going on. I've got a man sitting here trying to finish an important conversation. I'll talk to you later, OK?'

He put the phone down quickly. The American looked uncomfortable. 'I have to go to the can.'

'Your real name,' said Raven. 'What is it?'

'Ben Stepka.'

'On your feet,' said Raven. He unlocked the handcuffs. Stepka rubbed the weals on his wrists. Raven kicked the man's underpants and trousers across. 'Put them on!' he ordered.

Stepka obeyed, steadying himself against the end of the sofa. Raven pointed at the bathroom with the end of the Browning.

'You've got five minutes. And leave the door open. You're too fat to go through the window, anyway.'

He leaned against the wall, watching the bathroom door from the passage. Kirstie had a trick of seeming to go along with one of his stories, then appearing on the scene unannounced. He had to get Stepka off the boat in a hurry. The cistern was flushed and the fat man shuffled out, holding his trousers up. Raven herded him back to the sitting room.

'Put the rest of your clothes on!' He kept the fat man's belongings, putting them in a plastic sack with the air-pistol and pellet. Daylight was showing through the chinks in the curtains. Morning broke without snowfall for the first time in a week.

'Where did you leave your car?' said Raven.

'A couple of blocks away.' Stepka pointed vaguely in the direction of the pub. 'I don't know the name of the street.'

'We're going for a ride,' said Raven. He weighed the nickel-plated revolver in his hand. 'Number one, this thing is loaded. Number two, I'll shoot you if I have to. You've nowhere to go except with me.'

'I'm no hero,' said Stepka. It was true. He looked what he was, a fat man with grave problems.

'What were you supposed to do after you'd taken care of me?' Raven glanced round the room. Kirstie had a quick eye if she did turn up on the boat.

Stepka picked up his cigarettes. 'Call in as soon as the job was done. The guy's going to be waiting.'

'Stall him,' said Raven. 'Tell him that I never left the boat. That I'm still there. And listen, you'd better make it good.'

He stood over the fat man as Stepka composed a number. Raven stored it in his head. They waited as the number rang. Stepka was sweating heavily. He glanced up at Raven.

'There's no answer. He can't be there.'

Raven perched on the end of the sofa. 'Let's get something straight before we move. What I said about you having nowhere to go is the truth. Your only chance *is* with me. Do as you're told and you'll get the break. If you don't . . .' He lifted a hand and let it fall.

'What do you want me to do?' said the fat man. He was redfaced and frustrated. 'Wag my tail? For crissakes, I *know* what the score is!'

'Good,' said Raven. 'This is what we're going to do. We're going to take a drive in your car. Do you think your man will come here?'

Stepka made a face. 'Hell, no. He doesn't like putting himself in the firing line. He must have gone out for something. He'll be back. He's not going to move until he hears from me.'

'OK, let's go,' said Raven. He opened the door to the deck, leaving the sitting room lights on.

The city was wide awake now, traffic noisy along the Embankment. The two men walked side by side. The Browning was in Raven's coat-pocket but he knew that it would stay there. Stepka had run out of steam. They crossed the road towards Old Church Street. Stepka pointed at the Toyota. It was parked a hundred yards away from Patrick O'Callaghan's house. A few more steps and Raven could walk in there with the fat man. He imagined the lawyer opening the door to them, prepared for the postman. The look of alarm as Raven explained.

Raven used Stepka's keys to unlock the boot of the Toyota. There was nothing there but the spare wheel and jack. He checked the interior of the car, finding no more than a street map of London.

'You drive,' he said and gave the keys to the fat man. 'I've told you the way I feel. I'd be happy to see you rot in jail for the rest of your life. But I want the man behind you. If I have to let you off the hook to get him, that's the way it has to be.'

Stepka's face bore a look of cautious hope and gratitude. Raven fanned it.

'Walk away from me and you're a guy on the run for attempted murder and conspiracy to murder. On top of that, I've got your money, passport and airline ticket.'

The fat man stared through the windscreen. 'How many times do I have to tell you, all right, all right! But there's one thing you'd better be sure of. No matter what happens to me you're a bad risk for life insurance.'

'I always was,' answered Raven. 'Get this thing moving.'

They joined the flow of eastbound traffic, following the river as far as Westminster, then turned north towards Piccadilly. It was necessary to give the fat man something tangible. His fear was very real. They found parking space in St James's Square. Raven unfastened his seatbelt.

'We're going to book your passage home,' he said. 'I'll do the talking.' Raven removed the ignition-key and locked up the car. A look of surprise remained on his face as they walked.

'You've got a sore throat,' Raven warned. 'Smile if you can and be pleasant.'

The Pan-Am counters were busy. They waited their turn for a desk to be free. A trim blonde greeted them with a smile. Raven produced Stepka's flight ticket.

'My friend's unable to talk,' said Raven, touching his throat.

'He has to get back to the States tomorrow, preferably by way of Paris. Will you see what you can do?'

The girl punched some keys and viewed the result on the monitor screen. 'I can get him on tonight's flight,' she said, looking up.

'Fine!' Raven said easily.

She filled in a ticket. 'By the way, I'm afraid the seat is in a non-smoking area.'

'That doesn't matter,' smiled Raven. 'It'll be good for him.'

She looked up again, pen poised. 'Is Mr Fiore a citizen?'

'He is,' answered Raven. The fat man looked at his feet.

The hostess stamped the ticket and pushed it across the desk. Raven's hand was there first.

'Have a good flight, Mr Fiore,' she said. 'Heathrow, twenty-three hundred hours. Check-in time is an hour and a half before take-off.'

They left the Pan-Am building, Raven's touch solicitous on Stepka's elbow. Raven's pockets were loaded down with the Browning, air-pistol, Stepka's possessions and the handcuffs. A walking Black Museum, he told himself. Back in the car, the fat man slumped forward behind the wheel, taking his weight on his forearms.

'Relax,' said Raven. 'You're doing just fine.'

Stepka turned his head sideways. 'I've done time with guys like you,' he said bitterly. 'Guys who jump on your back and never get off!'

'You mix with a bad class of person,' said Raven. 'I don't usually make promises to people like you, but when I do I keep them.'

Stepka looked at his cigarette packet. There were a few left. He stuck one in his mouth and lit it from the lighter on the dashboard.

'That business with the ticket doesn't fool me,' he said. 'There's no way you're going to turn me loose and you know it.'

'Wrong,' said Raven. 'But first we've got to land the big one. That's part of the deal, remember.'

Stepka nodded heavily. 'That's what worries me. This guy's no fool. These people put their heads in the air, sniff a couple of times and they're gone. Where does that leave me?'

'He's going nowhere,' said Raven. 'They want me dead and they're not going to move as long as there's a chance of it. You're going to make another phone-call.'

Stepka put his hand on his sweating forehead. 'And say what?'

'It's simple; that you hung around, still waiting for me to

leave. It was already light and you couldn't risk me seeing you more than once. So you had to be careful. I left in a taxi about ten and by the time you got back to your car I was out of sight.'

'Are you being serious?' Stepka's stare was disbelieving.

'We both are,' answered Raven. 'You'll make it sound convincing. You're a good liar. Tell him you're still in Chelsea, you want to know what to do.'

The American closed the ashtray cover on his cigarette. 'Suppose he tells me to go back to the house. Are you going there with me?'

Raven shook his head. 'Don't be stupid, Ben. I don't know what I'm going to do with him yet. I'm betting that he'll tell you to stay where you are until I get back. You're expendable like the rest of them. You're just there to pull the trigger.'

Stepka's laugh was joyless. 'This is great stuff. Middle-aged and I still haven't learned.'

'But you're learning,' said Raven. 'Let's make this call.'

They crossed the square to the row of telephone-boxes. Raven crowded in with the fat man. There was barely room, even with the door ajar. Raven dropped a coin, heard the dialling tone and passed the receiver to Stepka. It was easy to follow the conversation. The voice Raven heard was the one that had called early that morning.

Stepka said his piece. His nervousness gave it credibility. He sounded a worried man, a man who had failed through no fault of his own. The other man heard him out.

'And where are you now?'

'Still in Chelsea. I've been trying to reach you.'

The smell of the fat man's body was rank in the confined space.

'And the car?' asked the voice.

'I had to move it,' said Stepka. 'It's a couple of blocks away. There are lights on the boat but I don't know if he's there or not.'

'OK, now listen! We'll have to change the scenario. There's a pub with a car park out front. It's almost opposite the boat. You can see the steps from there.'

'It's closed,' mouthed Raven. Stepka said it out loud.

'I know that. Move the car there as soon as the place opens and keep your eyes skinned. That's if you've made sure he's not aboard. You've got his telephone number. If he's not there, wait for him! Whichever way it is, the moment you're sure go down the steps. There's a door with an entryphone at the bottom. Ring the bell and say you've got a message from Hansen, H-A-N-S-E-N! He'll open up. The moment he does, let him have it and get the hell out of there. Now have you got that, Ben?'

Stepka rolled his eyes at Raven. 'He didn't go for that call this morning.'

'Something must have happened,' the voice said quickly. 'He'll answer. And don't forget, the moment he does, plug him. The rest is still good. Get rid of the gun and the car and call me. I'll wait here until you do.'

The fat man hung up and mopped his face and neck. 'Move over,' said Raven, 'And hold the door open!'

He dialled again and got Jerry Soo. 'Don't ask questions,' said Raven. 'Just be in Hyde Park in fifteen minutes. If you're not there I'll wait. The car park behind the restaurant by the Serpentine. I'll be in a grey Toyota.'

He pushed Stepka out of the booth and hurried him back towards the car. Stepka's breathing made it hard for him to speak. He seemed to be asking for approval.

'What do you think?'

Raven turned his head. 'I think you're wonderful.'

Hyde Park was empty save for some blue-faced schoolboys chasing a football, muffled couples exploring the fringe of the frozen lake and the usual Japanese with cameras. There was one other car in the space behind the closed restaurant.

Raven jerked his thumb. 'In the back seat,' he ordered. 'And keep quiet unless you're spoken to.'

He kept looking towards Queen's Gate. It was the route that his friend would probably take. It was twenty-five minutes before the black Rover turned into the parking area. Soo

DONALD MACKENZIE

emerged, sturdy and muscular, wearing a Gestapo-style rain-coat. He bounced across, boot-button eyes enigmatic as he climbed into the front seat of the Toyota next to Raven.

Raven opened his fist, displaying the air-pistol and flattened pellet. 'Do you know what this is, Jerry?'

The Chinese-born policeman bent his head low, taking a close look at the pistol without touching it. He straightened his back.

'Markov,' he said. 'The Bulgarian defector. Somebody filled him full of Ricin what was it, five, six years ago.'

Raven dropped the pistol in his pocket. 'How can you know these things?'

Soo smiled with false modesty. 'I have that sort of mind.'

Markov was a name that both men remembered. The Bulgarian had worked for the BBC Overseas Service. Waiting for a bus one morning he had felt a sharp jab in his thigh. He turned in time to see a man with an umbrella jumping into a taxi. Markov felt sick a couple of hours later. He went home and started to vomit. By the time the doctor arrived he was running a temperature of 103°. Admitted to hospital, his condition deteriorated rapidly. There was a drastic fall in blood-pressure. The doctor in charge diagnosed leukaemia.

Markov died the following day. The post-mortem revealed a tiny pellet embedded under the skin of his thigh. The cavity in the minute capsule was empty. Isolation of the substance it had held was impossible. A scientist from the Government Chemical Defence Establishment testified at the inquest that the poison was almost certainly Ricin. The coroner returned a verdict of 'Unlawful Killing' pointing out that Ricin was an antigenic. After a few hours in the bloodstream there was no way of detecting it in human tissue. It was the perfect assassin's weapon.

Raven nodded at the man. 'This joker's not a very nice man, Jerry. He's sorry he did not kill me. As it is, I'm his only hope.' Raven explained what had happened.

'George Drury's being cremated on Monday. I'm going to stop it, Jerry. If they burn George it weakens the case against

144

the people behind our fat friend. They're the ones who paid George's tax bill, the people who had him killed.'

Soo swung round, taking a good look at Stepka for the first time. 'You've got proof of all this, of course.'

Raven eyed him sharply. His friend's face told him nothing.

'I've got this guy,' said Raven. 'And I'm getting close to the others.'

Soo took his left fist in his right hand and cracked a couple of knuckles. 'I keep saying this, John; how long have we known one another?'

Raven smiled, sensing what was coming. 'Seventeen, eighteen years.'

'Eight of them since you left the force. And I've always gone along with you.'

'In a manner of speaking,' Raven admitted.

Soo leaned his stocky back against the car door, looking at Raven. It seemed as if he needed to make every word tell.

'I believe everything that you've told me, John. That's why I want you to walk away from it as of this very moment. Drop the whole thing. Go home and pack, get hold of Kirstie and Maggie and take the next plane out of the country. It doesn't matter where, just get going. And stay out until I tell you to come back. I'll take care of everything here.'

Raven swallowed carefully. Above all else he felt a deep sense of disappointment. He could feel the fat man's eyes on them, hear his heavy breathing.

'It's a funny thing,' said Raven. 'You're the last person in the world I'd have expected to give me that kind of advice.'

'And this time I know what I'm doing. This is serious stuff and you have no part in it, John. This is the Establishment. They'll destroy you if they have to, along with the people around you. Kirstie, Maggie, anyone! Get out before it's too late.'

'I don't believe this,' Raven said, reaching automatically for a Gitane. 'I had this stupid idea that we understood one another.'

'I understand *you*,' said Soo. 'I'm probably the only person in the world who's prepared to tell you what you don't want to hear. That's because I'm your friend. Look, John, if what you say is true, and I accept that it is, George Drury was a killer himself. Have you thought about that?'

'I've thought about it,' Raven admitted. 'He didn't have much choice, did he? And the man he killed was probably no loss to humanity.'

Soo's voice was tinged with regret. 'You and Kirstie mean a lot to me. I'm telling you what I think is best for you.'

Raven was touched by his friend's sincerity. 'I know, but I just can't do it. It isn't right, Jerry.'

Their eyes locked for a moment. Soo was first to break. 'Then you're on your own, John. You're making me say things I'd rather not say but I can't help you destroy yourself. I *won't* help you destroy yourself.'

'You may do whatever you feel,' Raven replied. He was losing something important in his life and there was nothing that he could do about it.

The Chinaman's smile came unexpectedly, a flash of gold-backed teeth. 'I know when I'm beat. Just do me one favour. Whatever it is you've got planned to do next just don't tell me. I've got enough on my conscience as it is.'

'You haven't got a conscience,' said Raven. 'You've never done a thing you regretted as long as I've known you. Nothing important, anyway. Forget Drury, think about me. This clown sitting behind us tried to kill me this morning. But he's just an instrument. It's the others I want. What are you suggesting that I do about it, Jerry?'

Soo pulled himself up from the door. 'I've already told you. As far as I'm concerned there's only one thing you can do.'

'And that's your final word?'

They stared at one another again, each striving to bend if not break the other's resolve.

'I'd lock you up here and now,' said Soo, 'if I thought I could get away with it. Anything to keep you out of the mess you're heading for. Yes, it's my final word.' He opened his door, walked round the front of the car and back to Raven's window. He stood for a moment, looking uncertain.

Raven wound down the window and gave Soo his hand.

'You're a hard man,' he said grinning. 'Take care of yourself, Jerry.' He remained looking after the Rover, long after the car had gone, wondering how much had gone with it.

'I'm out of cigarettes!'

The fat man's whine pulled Raven back to reality. 'Do you see what you bastards have done? he said, over his shoulder.

Stepka shifted uncomfortably. 'Your friend made sense. Maybe we should all run.'

Raven nodded. 'I could always be sure about you. The only thing that stops you doing a runner is the fact that you've got nowhere to go.'

He unfastened his door and cranked his long frame out of the car. He turned his head briefly. The fat man blinked and spread his hands. Raven walked across the tarmac to the restaurant. A waiter inside was setting the tables. Raven rapped on the glass. The waiter came across and opened the door.

'We're closed,' he said, indicating the sign on the door.

Raven pushed a five-pound note into the man's hand. 'I want a phone and a packet of cigarettes. Any sort will do.'

A few seconds were enough for the man to make up his mind.

'The phone's on the bar,' he said, pointing across the room.

Raven could see the Toyota through the window. Stepka was still there. Raven picked up the phone. The man he was calling was Ross Stewart, an old friend of Kirstie's.

A girl's voice announced '*Toronto Record*!'

'This is John Raven,' he said. 'Let me talk to Ross Stewart please.'

Stewart headed the London bureau of the *Record*, a glossy with a record for hard-hitting investigative journalism. His voice came on the line.

'Hi, John! It's been a long time. What can I do for you?'

'I've got a red-hot story for you if you're big enough to handle it,' said Raven.

'Really?' The other man's voice was less than enthusiastic. 'Can you give me a clue?'

'No clues,' said Raven. 'It's the package or nothing. And time's important.'

'I see.' There was a moment's hesitation. 'Where are you speaking from?'

'I'm in Hyde Park. Will you see us or not?'

'You say "we". Is Kirstie with you?'

'No she isn't. Is it yes or no?'

'OK, you'd better come here. Tell them at the desk downstairs that you're expected.'

The waiter had a pack of Marlboro waiting at the door. Raven walked across to the car, tossed the cigarettes at Stepka and put the ignition-key back in the lock.

'You're driving again,' he said.

The fat man took the wheel, a cigarette in his mouth, favouring his cut lip.

'Left round the park,' Raven instructed.

The offices of the *Record* were in Bond Street. A ramp led down to a subterranean garage. Fourteen floors of steel and concrete had been faced with terracotta. The piazza at street level housed an Arab bank, ethnic eating places and a variety of boutiques. A fountain played under artificial sunshine. Down below in the garage, support-pillars rose from half an acre of parking space. The words RESERVED FOR TORONTO RECORD were stencilled on the cement floor. Stepka drove over them. Raven locked up the Toyota. Both men walked across to the lifts. A uniformed security guard was sitting at a table nearby.

'For Ross Stewart,' said Raven. 'We're expected.'

The guard used the house-phone and jerked his head. 'Take the express. '

The cage rose rapidly, defying the law of gravity. They stepped out into a large, tiled hall decorated with dramatic photographs of Northern Ontario taken in winter hanging on the walls. A door opened and Stewart appeared. He was a big, good-looking man with fair curly hair and a misleading smile. The way was littered with the bodies he had trodden over on his way up. He wore an Italian jacket and high-waisted trousers that concealed the beginnings of a belly.

'Come on in,' he said heartily, cocking an eye at Stepka.

The room they entered was half the size of a tennis court. An interior designer with a big budget had designed a fantasy world high above the bustle of Bond Street. *Trompe-l'oeil* walls offered access to sunlit gardens. The furniture was modern Italian with silk rugs on the floor. Double-glazed doors opened on to the roof where trees that would blossom in May were protected by cloaks of aluminium foil. The television towers of Crystal Palace spiked the distant horizon. There was a green, leather-topped desk with matching chairs. Stewart closed the door and spoke into an intercom box on the desk.

'Send up some coffee. Three cups.'

He arranged himself comfortably in one of the chairs, waving invitingly. 'Sit down!' The two men sat. 'Who's this?' said Stewart, pointing at Stepka.

Raven ignored the question. 'You want this story or not?'

Stewart showed well-ordered teeth with the confidence of a man who is sure of his own personal charm.

'I don't know what the story is, John.'

'Well it isn't gossip-column material,' Raven answered. His wife had been engaged to Stewart when the three of them met. It was an engagement made precarious by differences of character. Raven had profited. They had continued to meet at parties, the two men avoiding one another pointedly. After six months of it Kirstie insisted on what she called civilised behaviour. The Canadian's self-assurance continued to make Raven's toes curl.

'You know who I mean by George Drury?' asked Raven.

'Who doesn't?' said Stewart. 'The Cockney lover. What's her name, Maggie Sanchez's boyfriend.'

'He's dead,' Raven said curtly. 'Blown up in a car outside Dorking. I've got proof it was murder.'

'Have you?' said Stewart. A hockey-puck travelling at ninety miles an hour had scarred his forehead.

Raven's smile was sarcastic. 'You're showing a great deal of enthusiasm.'

'What's the matter?' said Stewart. 'Are you sensitive all of a

149

sudden? You've got proof that someone was murdered so go to the police.'

Whatever else, Stewart had the fire-power Raven needed. The London bureau covered the whole of Eastern Europe and Stewart had friends in both high and low places.

'Let's get something straight between us,' said Raven. 'As far as I'm concerned, you'd never come first in a popularity poll and you hate my guts. That's fine, but this is business.'

'I don't know what you're talking about,' Stewart said easily. 'I see you as someone who came along at just the right time for Kirstie. She never really wanted to marry me. Then you arrived on the scene. I'd like to think that you make one another happy and that's about the extent of my interest. So you see you *are* getting sensitive.'

The chair was small for someone of Stepka's girth and he looked uncomfortable.

The Canadian's statement was delivered with eyeball to eyeball frankness and Raven believed not a word of it. He knew that Kirstie still met Stewart for the occasional drink and the *Record* used her work from time to time. She made no secret of it.

'You say go to the police,' said Raven. 'Suppose I told you that the police are part of the conspiracy?'

A frown puckered the scar on Stewart's forehead. 'What conspiracy are we talking about?'

'A conspiracy to conceal the fact that American spooks are operating in this country.'

The Canadian was tapping the top of his desk with a letter-opener. 'Who do you mean, the CIA?'

'I don't know,' Raven confessed. 'But they're American and they've got the Establishment behind them. The police and the Home Office.'

Stewart lifted the letter-opener. 'Hang on! You're saying that American secret servicemen are operating in the UK with the approval of the authorities?' He seemed determined to spell things out.

'Consent if not approval.' Raven's fingers closed on the

air-pistol in his pocket. 'I can give you proof of it.'

'Horseshit!' said Stewart. He threw out an arm with abandon. 'Sure there's a CIA presence, a station at the embassy. They do their business with the people here. Exchange of information and so forth. They're supposed to be on the same side, for crissakes. But *murder* – no chance! Let me tell you where Mrs T gets her advice when it comes down to heavy security matters. She gets it from the Cabinet Joint Intelligence Committee. And do you know who sits on that committee? The commander of the SAS regiment. There's no way that the SAS would hold still for American spooks running loose over here!'

Raven looked at him. The way the Canadian said it made a nonsense of Raven's statement.

'I don't care where she gets her advice,' Raven said obstinately. 'Maybe she's never been told.'

Stewart came to his feet and walked as far as the windows. He stood for a while gazing out across the roofs and then turned.

'I don't want you to get this wrong, John, but from what I hear you've been on the rampage ever since you left the police force. Striking terror into the hearts of evil-doers. A kind of Captain Midnight.'

Raven was losing his temper. 'A remarkable assessment! Who's responsible for it, my wife?'

'No!' laughed Stewart. 'Absolutely not! She still seems to think you're wonderful. I'm talking about the people who *really* know you.' He turned his attention to Stepka. 'I hope this isn't boring you?' he asked politely.

The fat man said nothing.

Someone knocked on the door. A girl came in with a tray carrying a Thermos flask of coffee and three cups and saucers.

'Milk and sugar's already in,' she said brightly.

Stewart used his charm on her. 'Thanks, Debbie. I don't want to be disturbed. Will you tell them downstairs?' The door closed behind her.

Stewart's yell brought her back. 'Check with the library. See what they've got on some people called George Drury and John Raven.'

She closed the door again and Stewart smiled. 'OK, John. What's the story?'

Raven pulled the air-pistol from his pocket. He placed it on the green-topped desk and added the flattened pellet.

'You should have asked her to check the library for what they've got on someone called Markov. The Bulgarian defector, remember?'

The Canadian's smile faded. 'What the hell are you talking about?'

Raven returned pellet and gun to his pocket. 'I'm talking about our fat friend here. He tried to kill me this morning, but don't worry about that. He and I have reached an understanding. In fact he's very fond of me, aren't you, Ben?'

Stepka's mouth opened and shut like a ventriloquist's dummy.

'Fuck you!' he said at last.

'He agrees,' said Raven, pouring himself coffee from the Thermos flask. 'You want the story, I'll tell you.'

It took him twenty minutes. Stewart's questions were to the point. Stepka confined himself to monosyllables, an animal tamed but still dangerous. The girl knocked and entered, carrying a sheaf of mimeographed pages. She put them on the desk in front of Stewart and retired. The Canadian paid them no heed. He waited until he heard the lift descending.

'What's your angle?' he asked, looking at Raven. 'I can't figure it out.'

'I wouldn't expect you to,' said Raven. Neither of the two men had touched the coffee. 'But let's call it lateral justice.'

'A nice phrase,' said Stewart. 'And you want us to help you apply it?'

'Right,' said Raven. 'You print in Canada. You can't be muzzled.'

Stewart was walking again, giving the fat man a wide berth as he crossed and re-crossed the room, using the space between the silk rugs as a promenade. Suddenly he stopped dead.

'It's half-past six in the morning Toronto time. DK will still be asleep.'

'Wake him!' said Raven.

The Canadian's face was uncertain. 'This is one time and place when we do things my way,' he warned.

Raven shrugged. 'Time is what we don't have much of. There's a man sitting on the end of the phone expecting to hear that I'm dead. He's not going to wait forever.' He knew about Duncan Kellog. In the six years that Kellog had owned the *Record* he had pushed the weekly magazine into the first place in Canadian investigative journalism.

Stewart was still undecided. 'Is it all right if we make a call?' asked Raven.

Stewart waved a hand. Raven dialled and crooked a finger at Stepka. 'You know what to say.'

The fat man stood splay-footed, sweating again. He swallowed hard and spoke.

'No sign of him yet. The lights are still on.'

The closed door and double-glazing trapped the sound of the voice at the other end of the line.

'What about his car?'

'It's still there,' said Stepka.

'OK,' said the voice. 'You know what to do. Call me as soon as there's news.'

Stepka waddled back to his chair and sat with his eyes on Raven. 'Satisfied?' Raven said to the newspaperman.

'I don't intend to make a goddam fool of myself,' Stewart said awkwardly. 'There are people downstairs whose jobs depend on my judgement. So does mine, come to that.'

'I'm not talking about jobs,' said Raven. 'I'm talking about the right and wrong.'

'Then try the Jesuits on Farm Street,' said Stewart. 'This is a newspaper office. And I'd take a story from the Mannheim mass murderer if it passed the test.'

'You mean mine hasn't passed the test?' Raven cocked his head.

'I mean I'm calling Toronto,' said Stewart. 'This is a rough business. Let DK make the decision.'

Stewart sat at his desk, the mimeographed sheets spread out

in front of him. He leafed through them, reading with the practised speed of the professional and dropping the discarded material on the floor beside him.

'Most of this is about you,' he said, looking up at Raven.

'I never realised you were such a celebrity. France, Switzerland, Portugal. You manage to turn something up wherever you go. I wonder how Kirstie keeps up with it all.'

'Patience,' said Raven. 'Or don't you remember?' If this was what it took to get Stewart's help, so be it.

Stewart was not prepared to let go. 'Hey, how about this! *Expelled* from France?'

'I was there last month,' Raven said calmly. 'We have an apartment in Paris.'

It was Kirstie's apartment and Stewart well knew it. 'What it is to have a wife with everything,' he said.

Raven eyed him steadily. 'Are you having fun, Ross?'

'You bet!' Stewart collected the sheets of paper into a pile and dumped them in the wastepaper basket. Then he picked up the cordless phone, wearing the look of a man who knows that he could get his head broken. He talked as he walked.

'I'm sorry about this, DK. Sure, I know what time it is. We could be on to something big over here but there are complications.'

He glanced sideways at Raven and Stepka and carried the phone to the window. He spoke with his back to them, his lips close to the mouthpiece. It was difficult to follow what he was saying. Finally he turned.

'DK's calling me back.'

'Calling you back for what?' Raven demanded.

'He's checking with Ottawa.'

'I don't believe this,' said Raven.

Stewart put the phone back on his desk. 'It's not too difficult. He happens to own the magazine.'

Stepka lit a cigarette as though his life depended on it. The three men sat in silence. The phone rang and Stewart reached for it. The conversation was brief.

Stewart raised his well-tailored shoulders. 'He doesn't want it.'

Disbelief stunned Raven's thinking. He had been prepared to answer more questions, for conditions to be made, but not for a flat refusal.

'He doesn't want the story,' said Stewart.

'Don't give me that rigmarole!' Raven found himself shouting and lowered his voice. 'You screwed me,' he said. 'And I know why.'

The Canadian loomed larger as though he'd inflated himself, the scar livid on his forehead.

'Why don't you wise-up, Raven? You're too old to be cutting these capers!'

It was the jibe that finally broke Raven. An insult from a blown-up gossip-columnist. Raven came to his feet, aware that the fat man was following his every move.

'You bastard!' he said. His whole body was shaking with rage and frustration. 'I'm holding you personally responsible. If I hear that a word of any of this has been leaked, I'll deal with you personally and you'd better believe it!'

Stewart flung open the door to the hall. 'Get the hell out of here, Raven, and take your fat friend with you.'

Stepka stumbled after Raven. If anything he looked relieved. Raven pressed the EXPRESS button. The door behind them slammed as the cage began its descent.

13

Loovey was at a window in the hall, watching the street beyond the bare trees. A removal van was parked twenty yards away, in front of an empty house. Men in white overalls were carrying in furniture. A woman in a fur coat and head scarf followed the operation with fluttering hands. Her dog was spraying the snow yellow, marking out new territory. Loovey surveyed the scene with indifference. His personal concept of home was a door he could open and shut. Possessions, for him, were a tyranny. Restless, he returned to the sitting room and the view of the river at the end of the garden.

His mind dwelt on Stepka, lurking somewhere near Raven's houseboat three miles downstream. Loovey was sure that Stepka would finish the job successfully. He had the attributes of a killer and had proven it. An indifference to the life of others, a readiness to snuff it out, weighing the risks against the reward. 'A psychopath given to illogical procedural patterns.' So read the jargon on his parole papers. In other words a fat slob who was prepared to kill.

The need to deal with Raven had become Loovey's overriding consideration. The fact that Raven had not used his car to go to the rendezvous indicated a fear of being followed. If he *had* gone it would have been by taxi, and the non-appearance of the man he was supposed to meet would have increased his suspicions. In any case he was bound to come back to the boat at some stage.

It would have been easier to whack him out in conventional fashion. An army sniper's rifle fired from the car park for instance. But that would have meant repercussions from the British and Arnold was in no mood to make more concessions.

It was a prospect that worried Loovey. Raven had friends, this lawyer for instance, people who would pursue the fact of a violent death. The idea of using Ricin as a means of killing had been with Loovey ever since he had read about it. The astute reasoning of an English doctor had been circularised throughout the station. The particulars given had impressed Loovey deeply.

Used in the right circumstances Ricin was the ideal instrument, a deadly substance untraceable after twenty-four hours in the bloodstream. He had kept his thoughts to himself. A few months later he had taken his requirements to a gunmaker in Liége. The gunmaker had supplied the weapon and pellet. A Malawi chemist in Brussels produced the poison.

Loovey tapped out a cigarette from the pack on the table. The looking-glass mirrored his image. His face showed none of his inner tension. Doubt still wormed in his brain. *The pellet*! It was the pellet found in Markov's body that had alerted the pathologist to the possibility of poison. Even then they hadn't been sure. But if the pellet was removed ... He shook his head unconsciously, thinking that he should have told Stepka. Instinct told him that it was something the fat man would never be able to handle. There was only one thing to do, complete the job himself. He opened a drawer in the kitchen and selected a small steel paring-knife. Its edge was ground to surgical sharpness. He wrapped it in a napkin and stuffed it in an inside pocket.

He heard the muted buzz of the scramble-phone, hurried into the sitting room and unlocked the wall-safe.

Fentiman's voice carried the faint echo of a call beamed by satellite. 'What the hell's been going on over there, Loovey? I've just been talking to Ottawa. Someone asked the RCMP for clearance on a story coming out of London!'

'Yes, sir,' Loovey said guardedly.

'Don't "Yes sir" me,' Fentiman snarled. 'The guy who asked is someone called Kellog. And you know what he does, Loovey? He publishes a Toronto magazine called the *Record*.'

The name tolled a faint bell. 'I've heard of it. Some kind of scandal-sheet.'

'A scandal-sheet, huh?' Fentiman's tongue rasped like an abrasive. 'You're talking about an outfit that put's more people out of business than the bankruptcy law. Nobody's safe from the bastards, including Margaret Trudeau.'

Loovey was puzzled. Fentiman couldn't be sinking his putts, or maybe his ex-wife was giving him a bad time. Quite simply Loovey did not understand.

Fentiman went louder and higher. 'Raven's been in the London offices of the *Record* offering a story about your activities over there. He's got times, places, and a version of Drury's demise that's too damn near the truth for comfort.'

It was as if some part of Loovey's brain had been awaiting the news. The words ballooned soundlessly from his mouth.

'Are you listening to what I'm saying?' shouted Fentiman.

Loovey managed to get it out. 'I'm listening, yes, sir.'

'Then answer, goddammit! Say something!'

Loovey pulled himself together. 'The situation's under control, sir.'

'Are you telling me you knew about this?'

'I made allowances for it,' said Loovey. 'Everything's under control.'

'It is, is it?' Fentiman's stopped his voice down to dangerous quietness. 'What we've got here is an ex-Scotland Yard man loose in London with a story that can sink the lot of us and you're telling me that everything's under control?

A tennis ball had stuck in Loovey's throat. He dislodged it with difficulty. 'You left it to me to deal with Raven and that's exactly what I'm doing, sir. It's a matter of time, that's all. A few more hours at most.'

'I thought you had him under surveillance. How come he can walk into a magazine office and you not know about it?'

The answer was less than flattering. 'He managed to slip the tail. With respect, sir, the man is hardly a beginner.'

'Damn right,' Fentiman said feelingly. 'I've got a copy of his file in front of me. Box Eight-fifty showed a little co-operation for once.'

Box Eight-fifty was a term used for MI6. 'It's just a matter of time,' Loovey repeated.

The other man sounded unimpressed, making a wet, clicking noise with his mouth. 'The RCMP knocked the story on the head after getting in touch with us.'

'Raven won't last the day,' promised Loovey. 'I've got someone on it.'

'Then take him off as now,' answered Fentiman. 'I don't care what you have to do, but take him off. Close the house up and get yourself back here the quickest way you can. That's an order, Loovey. Understood?'

Loovey saw his career collapsing about him. Seven years of dedicated service. He summoned the last of his reserve.

'Just one minute, sir. You owe me that much at least.'

'A minute for what? You screwed it up, Loovey. That's all there is to it.'

But it wasn't. This was the difference between disgrace and the spring-heeled bound that would carry him out of the snakepit. He put his case desperately.

'You gave me an assignment, sir. A difficult one. And I carried it out successfully. If there are loose ends left it's my duty to tie them up.'

'I'll tell you what your duty is,' Fentiman answered. 'Your duty's to do as you're goddam well told.'

Loovey took a deep breath. 'A chance, sir,' he pleaded. 'Is there any way that Raven could know that we're on top of him? I'm talking about his visit to the *Record* offices.'

'I've already told you, the RCMP knocked it on the head. Obviously they'd have been in touch with their people in London but all the *Record* knows is that the story's not for publication.'

'Then you can forget Raven,' said Loovey. 'I need this chance.'

It seemed a long time before Fentiman answered. 'You're an obstinate sonofabitch, Phil, and I shouldn't be doing this. There's a report sitting on my desk waiting for signature. I guess I can sit on it for a few more hours. You've got until midnight your time. If I don't have the right news by then the report goes to the Director.'

'I'll stake my reputation on it,' said Loovey.

'You just have, Phil,' said Fentiman. 'Midnight.' He cut the connection.

Loovey looked at his watch. It was two o'clock. Ten more hours. He used the scramble-phone again. He dialled New York and identified himself.

The answering voice had the peppy sound of a salesman. 'Hail the King! How about that! How's the weather over there?'

'Lousy,' said Loovey. 'Are we on tape?'

'Sure are,' the voice said cheerfully. 'Regulations, and you know how we strive after perfection. What can we do for you?'

'Is Drexel available?' Loovey knew the man. He was totally reliable.

'He's up in the Adirondacks. Just got back from a field assignment.'

'Can you get hold of him?'

'I guess so. We've got an emergency number.'

'Get him,' said Loovey.

A series of clicks followed, a ringing, then a voice came on the line. 'Drexel.'

'It's me, Phil! Listen, I've got a problem. There's a guy flying back to the States tomorrow. I'll give you the details later. He's got a big mouth, Hank, know what I mean?'

'Yeah, I get it.'

'He's travelling on a US book, name of Salvatore Fiore. There's a picture of him on file in New York in the name of Benedict Stepka. He's white, forty-seven years old and goes around two hundred and forty pounds. In other words, he's fat. This is a bad one, Hank, and he's got to be stopped.'

'I think I know who you mean,' said Drexel. 'Isn't that the good old boy from the south?'

'The same,' said Loovey, 'and he's got to be cashed. He'll be heading for the Harbour Hotel in Stonnington, Connecticut. His wife's staying there. How soon can you be in New York?'

'I don't know. A couple of hours if the airport's open. What do you want me to do?'

'Get hold of the Boccardo brothers. They're stand-up people and they've got that fast boat. They can sink Stepka somewhere west of Rhode Island.'

'I'll call them right away and arrange a meeting,' said Drexel.

Relief flowed over Loovey's brain. 'The guy's been working with me over here, Hank. And I've got an idea he's thinking of taking his own act on the road. He's got to be stopped. Tell the Boccardos to take the wife too. Stepka might have confided in her. Whatever's found on them is to be held for me. I want to know what's under their fingernails. OK?'

'OK, I'll get on to it right away.'

'And, Hank! We don't want the state police involved. This has got to be handled discreetly.'

'My pleasure,' said Drexel. 'By the way, I heard a rumour that Battaglia's no longer with us.'

'People talk too much,' said Loovey. 'Thanks, Hank, I'll return the compliment one of these days.'

He locked the safe and walked through to the kitchen. Once he and Stepka had left, the house would be thoroughly cleaned, surfaces polished, rubbish emptied, fresh linen on the beds. One hundred Hurlingham Drive would revert to what the incurious neighbours assumed it to be, the home of an absentee owner who occasionally lent it to friends. Loovey's mind still ran on Stepka and Raven. As long as either of them stayed alive there was the risk that the Battaglia file could be re-opened. And as long as the risk existed, Loovey's future would be in jeopardy. The situation was worsening by the hour and he knew what was at stake better than anyone. Above all, he feared the life he would be forced to lead outside the Company. He had come straight from school to the world of shadows where names, activation and identities were matters of convenient invention.

The heating registers clanked on the sitting room walls. The atmosphere was stifling. He adjusted the thermal control and opened a window. The clanking stopped after a while and the house lapsed into uncanny stillness. He lit a cigarette and sprawled out on the sofa. As soon as he'd gone through the customary debriefing he'd take a month's leave and do what he liked doing best. There were still places in the Pyrenees where you could ski virgin slopes, mountain lodges that offered comfort and privacy.

It was ten past four in the afternoon when the black phone on his chest came to life. The fat man's voice was guarded.

'He's just back in a cab. He's with another guy. I can see them both. The curtains aren't drawn.'

Loovey struggled upright on the sofa. 'Where are you speaking from?'

'I'm in the pay-phone at the bottom of Old Church Street. I had to move when the pub closed. I was the only one left on the car park.'

'What does the other guy look like?'

'Thirty-five, forty. On the short side.'

'Can you see what they're doing?'

'Not right now. I'm standing round the corner. They were talking, not a care in the world. You know, *normal*.'

'What does the rest of the scene look like?'

'Cool,' said Stepka. 'People coming and going along the street but the boats are quiet. The car's still in the alleyway.'

'OK,' Loovey said quickly. 'Don't worry about a thing. I'm going to call him right now. He knows my voice. I'll explain that something came up this morning, but I'll be on the boat at seven o'clock tonight. You've got everything ready?'

Stepka's voice tightened a couple of notches. 'In my pocket.'

'Then here's what you do. At seven o'clock precisely, you go down those steps and ring the doorbell. Don't use the entryphone. No conversation. He'll be expecting me so he'll open up. If he sees you through the window just keep going. Carry something in your hand as though you're delivering it. Hit him the moment you're close enough and try not to do it outside on the deck. And make sure the drapes are pulled when you leave.'

'Suppose the other guy's still there?'

'He won't be,' said Loovey. 'Leave that to me. How far is your car?'

'It's just up the street on a meter.'

'Stay in it,' said Loovey. 'And don't leave the neighbour-hood. Just sit in the car and wait. I'm relying on you, Ben.'

'You've got it,' said Stepka.

Loovey's smile was satisfied. Greed was the fat man's badge of courage.

'My bag,' said Stepka. 'What happens to my bag?'

Loovey glanced over his shoulder. The flight-bag was on the stairs.

'Forget it,' he said. 'You've got your passport and money. Buy yourself a toothbrush. New York's full of clothes. And remember what I told you. Get rid of that stuff in your pocket, bury the car and call me here.'

'What happens then; do we meet?'

'We meet,' said Loovey. 'Now do it right, Ben.'

Loovey swung his legs to the floor. He'd finally cracked it. The guy with Raven could be another newspaperman but Loovey doubted it. Raven wasn't the type to back a loser twice.

14

Raven hurried Stepka across the street to the Toyota. This time Raven took the wheel. He drove fast in spite of the slippery road surfaces. The fat man slumped in the seat beside him, staring through the arcs made by the windscreen wipers. The last few hours seemed to have shattered him.

'You're getting better all the time,' said Raven. 'You ought to be doing this professionally.'

Stepka wiped his mouth. His lip was troubling him.

'I've got a target as big as a house hanging on my back,' he said. 'They're not going to let me live.'

'They'll have to find you first,' Raven answered, trying to pump a little resolve into the other man.

It was only just after four o'clock but lowering clouds already squeezed out the light. The street lights were shining. There was parking space at the bottom of Old Church Street. The two men walked around the corner on to the Embankment. They hurried down the stone steps to the gangplank. The phone started ringing as Raven opened the door on the deck. He grabbed the receiver. The voice by now was familiar.

'What kind of game do you think you're playing?' said Raven, signalling Stepka to close the door. The fat man moved ponderously.

'There were reasons. Are you alone?'

'I'm alone.'

'You still want to know the truth about your friend?'

'The truth, yes. I don't want to play any more games. Who are you, anyway?'

'All in good time,' said the man. 'Be on the boat at seven o'clock and you'll get all you need.'

Raven slid down on to a chair. 'What's that supposed to mean – "all I need"? Drury's dead.'

'You know what you want. You may not get justice but you'll get revenge.' The man sounded like someone playing an unbeatable poker hand.

'And you. What do you get?'

'Satisfaction,' said the voice. 'Satisfaction and the sort of money I know you can afford. 'Oh, and listen! I don't want company. Make sure you're alone.'

It was twenty past four by the clock on Raven's desk. The gamble was launched. He dialled Patrick O'Callaghan's office.

'This is it,' Raven said urgently. 'Jump in a taxi and go round to Maggie's. Don't let them move if you're there before me. I'm leaving now!'

He opened the door to the deck. Stepka followed like a faithful hound. Snow had started to fall again, cool and soft in their faces. They climbed the steps and sidestepped through the traffic to the Toyota. Raven took the wheel. He looked at the fat man before starting the motor.

'You're scum,' he said distinctly. 'But if this thing works, I'm letting you run for it.'

Stepka's mouth opened. The reflection of light showed his eyes fixed on Raven's face.

'Don't say it!' warned Raven. 'Just don't say it!'

He shifted into first and they drove in silence. O'Callaghan was paying off a taxi as the Toyota turned into Cresswell Place. He waited for them to join him, a slight figure with his overcoat collar hiding the lower half of his face. Raven touched his arm and lifted the door-knocker. A light came on in the hall.

'Who is it?' said Kirstie.

'Open up, it's me,' answered Raven.

She stood, framed in mellow light, her blonde hair tied with a ribbon. Her face was devoid of make-up and she was wearing the black suit she had brought from Paris. Her gaze rested on Stepka.

'He's with us,' Raven said, pushing the fat man into the hall. Raven pointed into the sitting room. Maggie was on the sofa, dressed in a simple black dress. A topaz ring that Drury had given her was her only jewellery.

Raven bent down and kissed her cheek. Grief had augmented her striking looks, hollowing her enormous eyes, stretching the ivory skin between her high cheekbones. He sat down beside her and took her hand firmly in his. Kirstie and the laywer had found chairs and were sitting. The fat man remained on his feet, looking at Raven uncertainly.

'Get a chair,' ordered Raven.

The fat man unbuttoned his overcoat and lowered himself gingerly.

'OK,' said Raven. 'Nobody talks until I've finished. There's a lot to do and we don't have much time. George was murdered and our friend here knows who's responsible.'

Maggie raised her head, fixing her eyes on the fat man. Her hand started to shake. Raven squeezed it hard.

'You're going to hear things about George you won't like,' he said. 'But none of them alter the fact that he was murdered. That's what we have to remember.'

A tap dripped in the kitchen, loud in the sudden silence. Maggie drew a deep breath.

'I'd like a glass of water, please.'

Kirstie got it for her. 'Thank you,' said Maggie. She took the glass, making an effort to hold it steady.

'Right,' said Raven. I'm going to put you in the picture. I want you to hold fire until I've finished.'

Kirstie sat on the other side of Maggie, close to her as Raven talked. O'Callaghan chain-smoked. Stepka's eyes never left Raven's face.

'OK,' Raven said finally. 'Tell them it's the truth, Stepka.'

Stepka just widened his hands.

Maggie's right arm flashed like a cobra striking. The glass she had drunk from smashed against the wall above Stepka's head. Raven grabbed her arm, holding it firmly until he felt her quieten.

'What sort of animal are you?' she asked bitterly, looking at Stepka.

He shrugged, returning her look as though they were alone in the room. 'What the hell do you know about it, lady? It's a different world out there.'

Maggie shook her head, clinging to Raven. 'I just don't understand,' she wailed. 'There was no need. Whatever I had was George's.'

'Then you didn't really know George,' Raven replied. 'That wasn't his style. Men don't live on women where he came from. You were the last person George could have gone to for help; don't you see that, Maggie?'

Raven took the air-pistol and pellet from his pocket and placed them on the table in front of the sofa.

'Let's talk facts,' he said. 'Two men are dead and I'm lucky that I'm still alive. Yet nobody wants to know. The whole weight of the Establishment is covering up for the people responsible. The police, the press and the Home Office. They said that it couldn't happen here but it has.'

Kirstie found her voice. 'I just don't believe it, not here in this country. There must be something that can be done.'

Raven craned forward so that he could see her. 'OK, suppose you tell me what!'

She stared back, white-faced except for the band of freckles across the bridge of her nose. Raven appealed to the lawyer.

'This character sitting over there comes into this country on a false passport.' He produced the document and held it aloft. 'The immigration authorities let him through, so does Special Branch. Ask yourselves *why*! Suppose I call the police now and tell them who we've got sitting here. I'll tell you what would happen. They'd be round here in five minutes and that would be the last we would hear of him. And this is England, not Russia!'

O'Callaghan ran a thumbnail through his moustache. 'I still think you're exaggerating.'

'You do, do you?' Raven found the term an affront. 'How about the Coroner's Court and the hospital. This bastard tried to *kill* me, Patrick. Or is that an exaggeration?'

He turned to the woman sitting beside him. 'Do you believe me, Maggie?'

'I believe you,' she answered quietly. 'That's what makes it so terrifying.'

167

O'Callaghan lit a cigarette, narrowing his eyes as the flame neared his moustache.

'Does Jerry Soo know about this?'

'Of course he knows!' Raven answered. 'But what do you expect him to do? He's trapped in the system. We don't even have the right to ask him for help any more. You're the only one who can do anything, Patrick.'

The lawyer's hand dwelt in mid-air, still holding the cigarette. All eyes turned on him, including Stepka's.

'*Me*?' he said.

'That's right, you. You wrote an article last year for the *Law Journal*, something to do with Magna Carta.'

O'Callaghan looked for an ash-tray, plainly embarrassed. Raven continued. 'I read it, remember! The fourteenth clause. "To no one will we sell, to no one will we deny right or justice." And a judge wrote you a letter of congratulation. I read that too.'

Understanding dawned on the lawyer's features. 'Lord Parrish. Come on, it was a polite note, that's all. Hardly an accolade.'

Raven rammed the point home. 'Didn't he call you a traditionalist?'

'Something like that,' the lawyer was suddenly wary.

'That's what you told me at the time,' observed Raven. 'And Parrish is one of the most respected judges in the country. A man who cares about the law, a man who loves England. I don't think there's anyone strong enough to hold him down. I believe he'd help us if he knew the facts, Patrick.'

Stepka's breathing was heavy. The lawyer looked at him with open dislike. 'Come off it, John,' said O'Callaghan. 'You're talking about a High Court judge.'

'Exactly,' said Raven. 'And justice is what it's about. We're being denied due process of the law and that's against everything Parrish stands for.'

The lawyer shied like a horse at a pig-pen. 'What are you suggesting, that we knock on his door and ask to see him? It wouldn't work, John, believe me.'

'It *can* work,' Raven argued. He pushed the long hair from

his eyes. 'We call him and ask if he'll see us. Just as long as we get the chance to talk. You can do it, Patrick. The man knows you. The least you can do is give it a try.'

Kirstie spoke for the first time in a while. 'I think John's right, Patrick. If you won't do it, I will.'

'I will,' added Maggie.

The lawyer rose from his seat as if wondering why. 'You don't just phone a High Court judge, for God's sake! It isn't the way things are done.'

'Do it,' Raven insisted. 'If you don't want an audience, use the phone in Maggie's bedroom.'

The lawyer got as far as the doorway, then turned with a troubled face. 'You realise what this means. I'll probably be struck off.'

It was difficult to be light-hearted but Raven somehow managed it. 'Not with your golden tongue, not you. Tell him that he's our only hope, the only one out there who can help us.'

O'Callaghan started up the stairs. Stepka seemed to have lost all interest in what was going on around him. He sat with his ponderous buttocks overflowing the chair, staring at the carpet between his legs. Kirstie glanced at him briefly.

'What are you going to do if the judge won't see you?'

Raven balled his shoulders. No one knew better than he when the odds were stacked against him. Realisation provided an extra gear.

'I'm not sure,' he said, telling the truth.

'But you won't give up?'

He smiled. There was no point in replying. She already knew the answer. He watched the clock until he heard the lawyer coming down the stairs. One look at O'Callaghan's face confirmed Raven's fears.

'He can't – or anyway won't,' said the lawyer. 'You must go to the police, that's what he said. Once you've done that, then he'll see me.'

Raven looked at each person in turn, hoping that his task would be made easier. Maggie was twisting the ring on her finger. Stepka was sullen, the lawyer regretful. Kirstie was the only one he could read beyond doubt. He knew the expression too well, the deceptive calm before the eruption.

'I don't expect the rest of you to agree,' he said after a while. It was his wife he was really talking to. 'But I know what I'm doing is right.'

He gave them a chance to speak but nobody took it. The time was five past seven.

'On your feet,' he said to Stepka. 'OK, you'd better make this good. It's your only hope. You're going to make one last phone-call. You've done your job and you've just left the boat. You're using the same telephone-box, the one at the bottom of Old Church Street. He turned into devil's advocate. 'Where did you shoot me?'

'Stepka was sweating again. 'In the sitting room.'

'*Where*?' Raven insisted. 'In the leg, in the head – where?'

Stepka moistened his lips. A vein bulged in his gross neck. 'In the back. You saw me and went for the phone.'

'And then? This is important.'

Stepka sought inspiration. 'You were still on your feet. There was this vase, I clouted you with it. You were out like a light when I left the boat.'

'On the floor of the sitting room,' Raven prompted. The women's eyes were startled. O'Callaghan was following every word. 'You're sure that nobody saw you leave the boat and you're sure that you hit the target. Right between the shoulder blades. You're on your way now to get rid of the gun and the car.'

He dialled, and placed the phone on the fat man's lap. Stepka's head sank on his neck. His eyes widened as he strained for sincerity. A voice said, 'Hello?'

'It's done,' Stepka mumbled. His voice cleared. 'In the back. I had to lay him out. He went for the phone.'

'You're sure?' the voice insisted.

That fat man dredged indignation from somewhere. 'For crissakes, I was only inches away from the bastard. I don't know if he recognised me, but he went for the phone as soon as he opened the door from the deck.'

'Did anyone see you leave?'

170

'There was nobody there to see,' said Stepka. 'The boats were deserted. Nothing on the street except people in a hurry to get home. I'm still in Chelsea. I'm on my way to get rid of the car and stuff.'

'I told you to do that first.' The voice was tight.

'I wanted to let you know,' Stepka answered.

'Well do it now,' said the voice. 'And get yourself to the airport. I'll be in touch the day after tomorrow. If you're out of New York leave a number. You've done well, Ben. You won't be forgotten.'

The conversation ended.

Stepka sagged, pudgy hands covering his grey crescent.

'Straighten up,' said Raven. 'I hate to see a fat man cry.'

Stepka lifted his head. Hate stared at Raven's face.

'The address,' said Raven. 'The address that goes with the telephone number.'

The demand seemed to drain Stepka of the last of his life blood, weakening him so that his voice was a whisper.

'One hundred Hurlingham Drive. Near the river.'

Raven reached inside his pocket. 'Is this the key to the house? A red tag was attached to the ring. Stepka nodded. Raven dropped the key back in his pocket. He gave Stepka the passport, air ticket and money. He opened the door to the hall and jerked his head. Stepka stuffed his belongings into his overcoat, wasting no time on farewells. He paused, his bulky frame filling the street doorway.

'There's something I wanted to say. . . .'

Raven looked at him with complete contempt. 'Just get the hell out of here!'

He slammed the door and hurried back into the sitting room, a hand held up, blocking the criticisms that he knew would be aimed at him.

O'Callaghan spoke first, although mildly. 'I hope you know what you're doing.'

'Do you?' challenged Raven. 'It's all part of a gamble I have to take. Keeping my word to that bastard was part of it.'

'Suppose he reneges?' said the lawyer. 'Suppose he goes straight back and explains what's happened?'

171

Raven answered with complete assurance. 'That's the one thing that he won't do. He's burned his bridges. He's on his way now to the airport.'

Kirstie was still next to Maggie on the sofa. She removed the hand that cupped her chin, looking at the gun he had taken from his lumberjacket pocket.

'What are you going to do with that?' she enquired.

'I'm going back to the boat,' he said. 'I'm expecting a visitor.'

Maggie turned her dark eyes on him. 'I want to help.'

'You can,' he replied. 'We can all help one another. George was part of our lives. Whatever I'm doing is for him. We're four ordinary people, but if we stick together we can still beat the system.'

Kirstie spoke in a small voice. 'I need you alive, but I don't suppose that matters too much, does it?'

He took her face between his hands. 'You know how much it matters, Kirstie. But part of being alive is doing what I feel to be right.' He dropped the gun in his pocket again.

O'Callaghan drew a long breath through clenched teeth. 'You say you're going back to the boat. What are we supposed to do in the meantime?'

'Go ahead,' Kirstie invited. 'Tell us!'

'I want you to stay here until I call you,' he answered calmly. 'No more, no less.'

She gave a short, bitter laugh. 'We're standing in the presence of the Archangel Gabriel himself! My *God* I'm glad I don't have a child!'

Maggie and the lawyer glanced at one another, clearly embarrassed. 'That's an awful thing to say to someone who loves you,' Maggie said quietly.

'*Love*?' Kirstie almost spat out the word. 'What the hell does he know about love?'

'What about you, Patrick?' Raven addressed himself to the lawyer. 'What's your stance now?'

Kirstie came to her feet again, stiff with anger. 'For God's sake, John, I wonder that you have any friends left! You're an adrenalin addict determined to destroy yourself, and you want us to help you do it.'

He made one last effort. 'Listen to me, all of you. There's nobody on our side out there. *Nobody.* George is dead and somebody tried to kill me. I'm going to get the man who's responsible. He's going to stand up and tell the world loud and clear just who he is and what he does. I don't know how, on television maybe. If not here, somewhere else! But somehow I'm going to do it. All I want from you three is to give me support.'

Kirstie started to speak but he stopped her. 'I'm not talking to you. You've made your point already.'

She stood her ground, her face determined.'I thought you were talking to all of us. Unless I don't count.'

'You count,' he said. 'And I know a hell of a lot more about love than you think, Kirstie.'

She closed her eyes in defeat. 'I give up.'

'Let him do what he has to,' Maggie said quietly.

Raven indicated the air-pistol on the table. 'I'm leaving that in your charge,' he said to the lawyer. 'I'll call you just as soon as it's over.'

'It doesn't even make sense!' A pulse beat erratically in Kirstie's throat. 'You're going back to the boat for *what*? How do you know that this man will come there?'

'If he doesn't you'll have nothing to worry about, will you?' said Raven. 'He'll come. He's got to make sure that I'm dead.'

Kirstie's fingers fastened on his sleeve as he kissed her mouth. They lingered after he straightened up.

'Be careful,' she whispered.

Raven nodded. 'Call Jerry Soo and tell him what's happening.'

She looked at him as if for the last time. 'I'll do that.'

He touched Maggie's cheek. 'George was a good man, darling. Let's not forget it.'

The lawyer accompanied him into the hall. O'Callaghan's voice was too low for the others to hear.

'You're forty-three years old, John. Don't take foolish chances.'

Raven felt for the keys of the Toyota. 'I'm forty-four and I've got varicose veins. And they tell me I drink and smoke too much. Just sit tight and don't worry.'

They touched hands and the door closed on Raven. He made one stop at an Indian corner-shop and bought a can of cat-food. He buried the Toyota in an all-night garage and hurried the last two hundred yards on foot. Tidal water was spilling over the bottom of the stone steps. He left the door to the gangplank unfastened. Snow swirled round the tall lamp-posts. The boats wallowed on the swollen river like water-buffaloes. Seventeen of them, where people lived the lives of incurious villagers, making their social exchanges with guarded civility. With the exception of his green-bearded neighbour, all were united in disapproval of Raven. It was a disapproval he acknowledged and ignored.

He let himself into the sitting room and turned off all the lights except the Tiffany desk-lamp. He emptied a vase of freesias on the carpet, smashed the vase against the sofa leg and left the fragments where they fell. He opened the can of cat-food in the kitchen, tipped half the contents through the window and added water to the can. He returned to the sitting room and started walking backwards, dribbling the contents of the can on the wall and the carpet in two places, the second just outside the bedroom. The result was unpleasantly convincing. He pushed over the lamp on the dressing table. It fell to the floor, diffusing the light from there. He dropped the empty can over the side and threw his jacket at the sofa. He turned his head slowly, trying to view the scene through the eyes of the man that he knew was coming. There was little in his life he was sure of, but of this he was certain. The man would come. Everything bore out Stepka's story. The signs of a struggle, the trail of vomit left by a man crawling to his last refuge.

The phone behind him rang with sudden violence. Instinct told him who the caller was. The ringing continued as he walked through to the bedroom. He lay face-down, sprawled across the bed, holding the gun in his right hand, arm dangling out of sight of anyone standing in the doorway. The phone ceased ringing abruptly. Raven continued to lie where he was, heart hammering, waiting for the sound or sign that would release the coiled spring inside him.

15

Loovey's bag was in the hall. He had collected it from the hotel, returning the Cadillac at the same time. From now on he would be using public transport. He checked his watch. It was lunchtime in Washington. The thought of bleeping Fentiman in the middle of a meal gave him pleasure. He used the scramble-phone again, going through the switchboard and waiting until they located Fentiman.

'It's done,' said Loovey. 'Raven's been taken care of!' He could hear the noise of the traffic in the background. Fentiman was in his car.

'No witnesses,' added Loovey. 'No one around to make trouble.' Stepka was no concern of Fentiman's.

Fentiman swore. 'These goddam drivers! How long before the body's found?'

'No way of telling,' said Loovey. 'But there'll be no flak this time, and that's bankable.'

'What about that thug you've got over there?'

'He's off the payroll, said Loovey. 'I'll explain when I see you.'

A car horn blared, drowning the sound of Fentiman's voice.

'I didn't hear you,' said Loovey.

'I said you've done a swell job, Phil. And I want you out of there fast.'

'I'm on my way,' said Loovey. 'I'm taking a morning plane out of Paris. I'll be in Washington at fifteen hundred hours your time. I'll come straight to the factory.'

'I'll be there,' Fentiman promised. 'And listen, Phil, talk to nobody, including the British. *Especially* the British. If anything *should* go wrong, we deny everything. Could you hold that one together, do you think?'

'No problem,' Loovey assured him. 'Whatever happened to Raven is nothing to do with us. I'll see you tomorrow.'

There was a faint chuckle in Fentiman's voice. 'That was a stroke of genius, planting Joe the way you did. Even his nearest and dearest are going to find the spot hard to locate. A swell job, Phil.'

Loovey locked the scramble-phone in the wall-safe. Almost eight o'clock. Time to wrap up the package. He put himself in the position of the person who found Raven's body. He'd take care of whatever signs there were of a struggle. A fall would account for any damage done to Raven's head. He took the nine millimetre Beretta from the drawer and loaded the slip with lightweight ammunition. Stepka's bag was still on the stairs. Loovey picked it up, turned out the kitchen lights and stepped out into the garden. No one saw him make his way across the frozen turf to the gate that led to the towpath. He unlocked it. A cabin-cruiser, shrouded for the winter, strained at the end of its rope. Swirling snow veiled the lights on the far bank of the river. Loovey opened Stepka's bag and dropped the contents item by item into the water. The bag itself went last. He re-locked the gate and trotted back to the house. A radio-cab despatcher promised a driver in ten minutes. He was standing at the front door when the taxi arrived.

Loovey settled himself comfortably. 'Kings Road, Chelsea. You can let me off on the corner of Old Church Street.'

He was getting a charge out of closing Raven's file in person. The bastard had come close to ruining him. The driver slid the taxi to the kerb. Loovey paid him off. The foyer of the small cinema was crowded with patrons. The few pedestrians abroad walked with purpose, scarved, gloved and hatted. Loovey snapped the brim of his own hat and started walking south towards the river. Stepka would be on his way home by now. Loovey knew his style all too well. Loovey's feelings about the ex-con were impersonal. The disposal of Stepka was a matter of pure expediency. There were winners and losers. It was as simple as that.

The phone-boxes the fat man had mentioned were at the bottom of the street, wet and unused. Loovey fed a coin into the slot and dialled Raven's number. He let it ring unanswered for three full minutes before hanging up. He stepped outside. The lights of the pub along the Embankment made a bright patch in the darkness. He crossed on the pedestrian 'go' signal and hurried towards the boats. The mooring-chains chinked and ground. The people aboard were snugly isolated from the world outside. He paused for a moment at the top of the steps, looking down at Raven's boat. A glow showed behind the curtains. He slipped on his gloves and descended the steps. The door at the bottom was open. The gangplank swayed in front of him. He climbed it cautiously, using the guard-rope. Once on deck, he peered through a chink in the curtains. The glow came from a lamp on a desk. He tried the door to the sitting room, holding his breath as he turned the handle. It opened quietly.

Shards of a smashed vase lay on the carpet. The flowers it had held were scattered nearby. A trail of vomit on the floor of the passageway led from the sitting room to the bathroom. There was no noise on the boat but the groaning of fenders. He moved forward, following the trail on the floor to a bedroom beyond the bathroom. Light from an overturned lamp on the floor suffused the wall. Loovey paused in the doorway. Raven was lying across the bed, face-down as he must have fallen. Loovey took two strides towards him.

Raven lay on the bed, his ears probing the familiar pattern of sound. The success of his plan depended largely on his hearing. The door at the bottom of the steps was sixty feet away yet he heard the noise clearly. The door banged twice in the breeze and was silent again. He held his breath, a ghost following the intruder up the gangplank and along the deck. The footsteps were light and cautious. The sitting room door was opened and shut with care. Silence followed as the intruder took stock. Then the light, wary tread was resumed. It ceased in the bedroom doorway. Raven saw the man through veiled eyes, framed in the dressing-table mirror. It was the man he had seen at Capel Manor. He stood stock-still, looking down at Raven, his arms slightly raised as though preparing to catch some invisible object. Then a hand crept to his overcoat pocket. It emerged holding an automatic pistol. The movement was made with the sureness of an expert. Only the width of the bed separated the two men. The intruder's next move would determine that Raven was alive and not dead. There was no time for a challenge, a call to surrender. Raven rolled sideways, away from the mirrored reflection. Both guns were fired simultaneously. The intruder's shot smashed the mirror, his aim troubled by the movement of the boat. But Raven's target loomed large against the wall. He fired, still lying prone. The bullet entered the other man's neck below the jawbone, smashed through teeth and palate and lodged in the brain. The man remained upright for the space of seconds, his face frozen in surprise. Then life left his body quickly, bright arterial blood gushing from his throat and mouth. His hat rolled from his head and he dropped like a man on the scaffold, falling across the bed.

Raven lay as he was for a moment, legs trapped under the weight of the dead man's body. A sudden sensation of wetness repulsed him. His feet found the floor and he ran to the bathroom, staring down at his bloodstained trousers. He washed his hands, face and body and donned clean jeans. His ears still rang from the noise of the double explosion. Nothing had changed in the bedroom. Blood soaked the duvet. The dead man's hand still grasped the automatic pistol. His torn throat and matted hair made him unpleasant to look at. Raven steeled himself to search the body. He did it without disturbing the dead man's position. A goatskin wallet contained twenty hundred-dollar bills, three hundred and fifty pounds sterling and a small amount of Belgian francs. The American passport was issued in the name of Dane Marshall, born Cambridge Massachusetts, 1955. Tucked into the stamp-pocket of the wallet was a piece of paper. Raven removed it.

IN CASE OF ACCIDENT NOTIFY 280-6000 EXTENSION

24. BLOOD GROUP A POSITIVE.

The watch on the dead man's wrist was a thin gold Cartier. Raven returned the man's belongings to his pockets. He opened the door to the deck, letting out the stink of burnt cordite. A light wind was blowing the snow. The night had accepted the gunshots without question. He stepped backwards over the pieces of broken vase. It was essential that everything should be left as it was. When the air had cleared he closed the door to the deck again and took the phone to the sofa. He found Jerry Soo at home.

'I'm on the boat,' said Raven. 'Did Patrick tell you what was happening?'

'He told me,' said Soo.

'Well I've just had a visitor. The trouble is that he's dead, Jerry. He pulled a gun. It was him or me. I was the lucky one.'

'It's a point of view,' said the cop. There was no criticism in his voice. He might have been discussing the weather.

Raven sensed the concern behind his friend's manner. 'I'm sorry, Jerry,' he said. 'I shouldn't be dragging you into this.'

'What have you done about it?'

'Nothing as yet.' Raven crammed events into a hundred words or so.

Soo just listened. 'And what happens now?'

The door was still banging at the end of the gangplank. Raven screwed his face up.

'I was hoping you'd be able to tell me, Jerry.'

'I've been telling you for years and when have you listened?' said the Chinaman. 'What do you think I can do for you?'

'I want to know what's going to happen to me,' Raven said anxiously. 'I killed in self-defence. There isn't a jury in the world that would convict me.'

'True,' answered Soo. 'But there won't be a trial either. You won't get your chance on the soap-box, John. None of your fine indignation.'

'You're a hard man at times,' said Raven. 'The thing is, this guy's no errand boy. He's important. I've seen him once before, down in the country. He's the one who had George killed.'

179

'He's important all right,' Soo replied. 'I understand you turned the other one loose. What do you think that's done for George Drury?'

'You don't even listen,' said Raven. 'Nothing can help George any more. Things will probably stay the way these people want them to be. But there's one difference. There's someone who knows the truth. *Me*!'

'Trouble with you, you're a bad loser,' said Soo. 'Have you got a licence for the gun you just used?'

'I have,' answered Raven. 'And the gun was used for the purpose stated on it. Self-protection.'

Soo spoke with conviction. 'They'll take it from you. You want to know what's going to happen to you, I'll tell you. The body will be whisked away. I'm guessing at this part but it'll be removed somehow. You'll see no one you recognise. Just faceless people who happen to mean what they say.'

Raven's mouth was dry. He found saliva for it. 'And what *are* they going to say?'

'I'm guessing again but something on the order of you taking a long holiday with Kirstie. For all I know, Maggie too. If that's what they say you should do, then do it!'

Raven recognised the warning in his friend's voice. 'And how do I contact these people?'

A dog barked in the sudden silence, responding to some challenge that it alone heard. Soo's voice was quiet when he spoke.

'This isn't going to be easy,' he started.

Raven sensed what his friend was about to say. An orphan left on the steps of the Macfarlane Memorial Hospital, Soo had had to fight all his life to overcome poverty and prejudice. At the age of forty-four he was both loved and respected. It was an achievement that he did not want to jeopardise.

Soo found his voice again. 'All I'm asking is that you leave my name out of it. The man you want is called Arnold. You'll reach him on seven three four five five five zero. If he's not there they'll find him for you. Tell him who you are and what's happened. And whatever he says, John, do it. Will you promise me that?'

'I'm a better loser than you think,' answered Raven.

'And stay away from the law!' The warning was firm. 'Are Kirstie and Patrick still at Maggie Sanchez's place?'

The dog chorus continued outside. Yes, but they don't know what's happened.'

'Good,' Soo said quickly. 'I'll explain everything. I'm on my way there now. And, John, no police and do what I've told you. Call me as soon as it's done.'

Raven dialled the number that Soo had given him. A deep voice at the end of the line repeated it. Raven drew a long, deep breath.

'My name's John Raven. I live on a houseboat called the *Albatross*. I've just killed a man in self-defence, an American called Marshall. At least, that's the name on the passport.'

It was a while before the other man spoke again. 'Who gave you this number?'

'Someone who thought that I needed it. If you're who I think you are, you'll understand why I'm calling you and not the police.'

'I'll tell you what I do understand,' the voice boomed. 'You've been making a confounded nuisance of yourself. What's the matter with you anyway! You had ample warning but you insisted on putting yourself at risk. Your wife too, or hadn't you thought about that?'

'I've thought about it,' Raven replied. It had been a long day and he was getting sick of it. 'Let's get something straight. I'm British, this is my country and I've done nothing wrong. If you're going to give me a hard time you'll find that I'm not without friends.' The words had a hollow ring in his head.

The boom had a touch of resignation about it. 'You're all I was led to expect, Mr Raven. My difficulty's to know what to do with you.'

'I'm pretty sure you've got the answer to that one,' said Raven. 'I'm ready to co-operate if that's the right word.' His leg had started to ache.

'Sensible chap,' said the other man. 'Arrangements will have to be made and I need the facts. How many other people know of your involvement in this affair?'

'Four,' answered Raven. He gave no particulars.

'Are they discreet? Can you trust them?'

'Let me put it this way,' said Raven. They wouldn't want to see me in any more trouble.'

'Nobody wants to see you in trouble,' the voice urged. 'The objective is to get you out of it.'

Raven shook his head obstinately. 'My difficulty is getting people to believe me. But I think I can do it, given the right platform.'

'I'm sure you could,' the voice agreed. 'But we're talking at cross-purposes. You haven't informed the police, you said?'

'I was told not to do that!'

'You seem to be well-advised. There's only one person you need to explain things to and that's me. You've already done that. I know more or less where you live, Mr Raven, but fill me in exactly.'

Raven looked east through the chink in the curtains. 'The boat is the first in line coming from Battersea Bridge. It's got a white hull and a cedarwood superstructure. I've got my own access-steps down from the embankment. The steps are wide enough for a stretcher if that's what you had in mind.'

'Excellent. How's the street lighting?'

'The steps are between two lamp standards, the third and fourth coming from the bridge.'

'And the other boats?'

Raven looked in the other direction. 'Not a sign of life. They're all below deck.'

'Last question, and this is important. You're sure that he's dead?'

'He's dead,' Raven said shortly. 'Does this mean that you're coming for him?'

'Yes. It'll take a little time to organise, say half-an-hour. I'll phone when we're leaving. It would be better if you met us at the top of the steps.'

I'll be there,' said Raven.

He poured himself a stiff Scotch and water. The bedroom

carpet would have to be cleaned, something done about the duvet. Mrs Burrows's emotions were easily aroused. He went back to the phone and the sofa. The number he had found in the dead man's wallet answered immediately.

'Extension twenty-four,' said Raven. It was something he had to do for his own satisfaction.

The transfer was made and man's voice answered. 'Cultural Attaché's office. Harold Baum speaking.'

'I'd like to speak to Dane Marshall, please,' said Raven.

'Who is this speaking?'

'A friend. Just say a friend.' He heard the hollow sound as a hand covered the mouthpiece.

Then the voice was back. 'There seems to be some confusion here. You did say Dane Marshall, didn't you?'

'That's right.'

'That's what I thought. There's nobody here by that name.'

Raven finished a drink, waiting for the phone to ring again. It came to life and he picked it up quickly.

'We're on our way!'

Raven grabbed a torch from the kitchen and stepped out on deck, directing the powerful beam at the other boats. He saw no one. He ran up the steps and stood between the lamp standards, looking right towards Battersea Bridge. The signals changed, releasing a stream of traffic. A Daimler flashed its indicator and pulled in to the kerb. There were three men inside, two in front and one in the back. The doors opened simultaneously. The man in the back was in his sixties, wearing a shapeless tweed Raglan coat and no hat. His head was bald except for tufts of ginger hair above his ears. He wasted no time with introductions.

'Is this it?' he asked, nodding at the steps.

Raven shone the flash for the others. 'Take care. It's slippery at the bottom.'

The other two men looked as though they were cloned. Both wore blue raincoats. Both had the clean, close-lipped faces of servicemen. Navy probably, thought Raven. He followed them down the steps. The older man was first into the sitting room.

Heavy-browed eyes took the scene in quickly. He swung round to Raven.

'Where is he?'

Raven led the way to the bedroom. The smashed looking-glass reflected the body lying across the blood-soaked duvet. The man with the Raglan coat bent down, making a close inspection of the dead man.

'Yes,' he said briskly, straightening his back. 'Clean him up,' he said to the other two. 'Have you Band-aids, sticking-plaster?' he added to Raven.

'In the medicine chest. The bathroom.' Raven pointed.

The two of them walked back into the sitting room. Raven's Browning was on his desk.

'Is that the gun you used?'

'Yes.'

'And the other one?' The man was looking at the compressed-air pistol. Raven held the man's gaze. 'I thought you'd know about that. Our dead friend's colleague had a go at me with it early this morning.'

The man slipped the air-pistol into the pocket of his Raglan. He glanced down at the flattened pellet.

'That goes with it,' said Raven. He did his best to smile.

The scrap of metal followed the pistol into the man's capacious pocket.

'An unpleasant piece of work,' the man said. 'He checked in at Heathrow half-an-hour ago, bound for New York. He won't be stopped. Letting him go was a stroke of genius on your part. You know, you show flashes of ingenuity, Mr Raven.' It was his first smile and it came as though he meant it.

His eyes continued to rove, finally settling on the Paul Klee. He considered it briefly.

'I'm afraid I've never been able to understand abstract art,' he said.

Raven shrugged his shoulders. 'It's something you're not meant to *understand*. It's a question of colour and form.'

'We must talk about it some time,' said the man. 'You know

I've always found policemen boring, but you're certainly different.'

Raven was finding him easy to talk to. 'My wife thinks I should never have been a policeman.'

'They often do,' said the man. 'I mean women. Make judgements about their husbands' pasts. I'm sure there's a lot you could tell me.'

He turned sharply as one of the younger men came into the room. 'We've done what we could with him, sir. It's not too bad.'

'Then get him on his feet,' He came back to Raven. 'I wonder if you'd go aloft and let us know when the coast is clear. Use the torch.' He was smiling again as if the whole thing were some prank.

The torch found the glistening granite walls of the embankment overhead. The enormous blocks had been quarried in Dartmoor a hundred years before. Pigeons roosted on ledges. Nothing human moved. He climbed the steps to the wet pavement. The pub lights shimmered as though under water. He could see the traffic-lights in both directions. Red signals stopped the line of cars coming east and west. He stepped back and flashed his lamp three times at the boat below. The three men came into view at the bottom of the steps. The one in the Raglan was first, donning a pair of yellow gloves as he climbed. The other two carried the body between them. The hole in the dead man's neck had been covered with surgical tape. The face had been washed clean. The hat was jammed down low over the ears. Raven opened the rear door of Daimler, counting the moments until the traffic-lights changed again. The two men carried the body between them, feet dangling over the wet pavement. They climbed into the car, wedging the dead man upright on the back seat, one on each side. Raven slammed the door as the signals changed from red to green. The first car passed the Daimler. The driver behind the flicking windscreen wipers would have seen a man who had been in a fight or an accident. A man lucky enough to have friends who took care of him.

The man in the Raglan rubbed his gloved hands together briskly. 'That's all very satisfactory,' he said to Raven. 'I've no doubt we'll be meeting again at some point. To wrap things up, as it were.'

'I'm not sure I'd look forward to that,' Raven answered. He had a feeling that this man would be able to put a different aspect on the build-up to George Drury's death and its sequel.

'Oh, we'll meet,' the man said with assurance. 'When you come back from your holiday probably.'

Snow was settling on his bald head. His wink was deliberate.

'Have you ever been to Costa Rica?' he asked. 'It's a delightful place at this time of the year.'

Raven glanced sideways into the Daimler. The scene in the back had not altered.

'We were thinking more of the Caribbean,' he said.

'An excellent choice,' the man said heartily. 'In the meantime, try to convince your wife and your friends that none of this really happened. You'll have no trouble with the police, Mr Raven. Rest assured of it!'

He removed his right glove and offered his hand. Its pressure was light and warm.

'Nobody here by that name,' Raven said suddenly. His short laugh was unconscious.

The man bent shaggy eyebrows. 'I'm sorry?'

'Just something I heard,' said Raven.

The older man's face cleared. 'Of course. Very good! I suggest that you spend the night with your wife and Miss Sanchez. Goodbye, Mr Raven.'

He settled himself behind the steering-wheel, fastened his seatbelt and set the Daimler in motion. Raven watched the tail-lights until the Daimler passed from sight. He descended the steps with a feeling of total complicity. The rules had changed but he was still on the winning side. And now he could think of no better place to be than with Kirstie.

>>> If you've enjoyed this book and would like to discover more great vintage crime and thriller titles, as well as the most exciting crime and thriller authors writing today, visit: >>>

The Murder Room
Where Criminal Minds Meet

themurderroom.com